BOOK FAIR SECRETS

A Bookish Cafe Mystery Book 7

HARPER LIN

This is a work of fiction. Names, characters, organizations, places, events, and incidents are either products of the author's imagination or are used fictitiously.

Book Fair Secrets

Copyright © 2025 by Harper Lin.

All rights reserved.

www.harperlin.com

Chapter 1

The Bennet Rockford Convention Center of Fair Haven, Connecticut, might not have been as immense as McCormick Place in Chicago or the San Diego Convention Center, which hosts one of the largest comic-book conventions in the world every year. However, Maggie Bell thought that whatever Fair Haven's convention center lacked in space, it made up for in aesthetics and history. It was pretty. It was interesting. It was a single level with two massive showrooms connected by a corridor adorned with commissioned paintings and sculptures by artists from all over the country. Even a few of Fair Haven's own had their creations displayed for months at a time. Walking from one end of the building to the other was a soothing yet inspiring adventure in texture, color, motif, and composition, punctuated by the faint scent of varnish and clean plaster.

Every year the Bennet Rockford Convention Center hosted the book fair, and every year Maggie was among the first to enter the venue and spend all three days hunting for old books to bring back to the Bookish Café where she worked. The fair felt like Christmas had arrived early, and not only had she been extra good all year, but there would also be several local authors offering talks, signing books, and an evening meet-and-greet.

Normally, Mr. Alexander Whitfield, the previous owner of the Bookish Café, would have happily attended the meet-and-greet and told her everything in detail, from what the authors wore to whom he thought was a fraudster and who was a real literary genius. But Mr. Whitfield had passed away, a thought still painful to Maggie. He had been her best friend. Maggie decided it was her job to pick up the torch and attend as a representative of the Bookish Café.

As the date drew closer, her excitement grew so much that she sometimes found herself alphabetizing a shelf twice, simply because her mind wandered to the author talks, the smell of fresh-printed paper, and the hum of delighted readers. Even Poe, the dignified bookstore cat, seemed to sense her anticipation; he would curl on her lap whenever she paused to jot down titles she hoped to find.

"You want to use your vacation time to go to the book fair in town?" Joshua Whitfield, her new boss, asked one afternoon, his eyes partially squinted and a sly smile on his face.

When he first arrived after his father Alexander died, Maggie feared he would ruin the store or sell it outright, along with the rare books for twenty-five cents apiece. Instead, he had turned it into a lovely Main Street attraction and preserved the antiquities collection, minus the old books that Alexander willed to Maggie as a nest egg and payment for the years she not only worked for him but also cared for him like family.

Although Maggie thought of Mr. Whitfield as family, she saw Joshua differently. He was the complete opposite of his father. Alexander had been an avid reader in a worn-out sweater with a scruffy white beard. Joshua, by contrast, wore a tool belt almost every day with blue jeans and steel-toed boots, a sight that made Maggie's heart race more than she'd ever admit. Awkward from the word "go," she had been a bumbling idiot when Joshua first showed up, blushing and bumping into shelves and doorframes. Yet something had clearly changed her. She now chatted with customers, and her gorgeously decorated storefront windows had earned two blue ribbons from the Fair Haven Town Beautification Committee.

Although her introversion had lessened, it was not gone. Chatting with people who wrote books, not just read them, felt intimidating, but Maggie was determined to follow in Alexander Whitfield's footsteps.

"What do you think I'm going to do on vacation, travel?" she said as she pushed up her glasses. "I can go anywhere I want for the price of a good book. I don't even have to stay on this planet if I don't want to,"

"You've got me there, Mags. Of course you can have those days off. Take an extra day or two if you need to recuperate after all the excitement. Casper can handle things while you're gone," Joshua teased, tapping a paint-spattered thumb against a stack of receipts.

"I might just do that," Maggie huffed. She returned to the display window of the Bookish

Café. The theme she'd chosen was "Hidden Treasure," fitting for the gems she hoped to find.

That evening, she sprinkled the display with bronze-colored glass beads that glittered beneath the recessed lighting, then stepped back to see how the pieces caught the glow. Poe twitched his whiskers at the sparkle and batted a bead onto the floor before deciding the tower of classics was a better perch than any velvet cushion.

It was late summer, and tourist season was in full swing. Business was booming. Bibliophiles crawled out of the woodwork, some searching for that final book to complete a series, others for the next release by a favorite author, and a few like Maggie looking for a singular volume they wouldn't know they needed until they saw it. In the quiet moments between customers, she created a neat, handwritten wish list organized by genre, title, and the maximum amount she would allow herself to pay. She also left a few blank lines, just in case destiny offered a surprise.

She bought her weekend pass the moment they went on sale. Nervously, she checked the mailbox each day, worried someone might swipe it like a Social Security check. When it arrived, she breathed a long sigh of relief, hung it on the fridge for safekeeping, and admired it daily. Like an Advent calendar counting down to Christmas, she eagerly awaited her vacation. For the first time she would attend as an official representative of the Bookish Café and stay as long as she wanted. She might even chat with vendors—maybe.

Outfits were chosen, comfortable yet classy, and she had saved enough money to splurge on any special tomes. She located a street spot within walking distance of the center to avoid the parking lot fee. A healthy breakfast awaited, and trail mix Joshua considered stocking at the café sat in her purse to spare her from overpriced pizza slices and hot dogs.

Maggie had always gone alone to the fair. Alexander had invited her many times, but she declined, claiming the bookstore could not close. The truth was that she preferred slipping around unnoticed. Alexander struck up conversations with strangers, a prospect Maggie dreaded. Now that memory stung. She had been with him when he died among his beloved books. Although she took comfort in that, she still missed him fiercely.

When the first day of the fair arrived, Maggie was up before dawn. Her three-day pass and trail mix were in her purse, and comfortable walking shoes were on her feet. She looked chic in a long grey skirt, a pink sweater, and black sneakers. The sky had been bright blue for days, yet today a solid gray blanket hung overhead, and a cool breeze rattled the maple leaves along Main Street.

She climbed into her car and headed to the Bookish Café as a customer. Babs, the rockabilly queen of croissants, was already bopping around, the strains of an old-school rock guitar riff floating over the hiss of the espresso machine. Cinnamon, butter, and dark roast coffee scented the room. Anyone watching would think Maggie had been gone for months, not hours.

"Don't you look like the cat's pajamas," Babs gushed. "You might land a hot date or two at this shindig. What can I get you to jump-start your engine?"

"Just coffee, Babs. I'm so excited I can't eat," Maggie said. "I've been counting down for weeks."

"We are talking about the book fair, right?" Babs arched her black brows into her blond hairline.

"Yes. I know I'm a nerd," Maggie replied, rolling her eyes and pushing up her glasses.

"Are you kidding? You're the coolest bookworm I know. Here you go, and this one's on the house,"

Babs said with a wink, handing over a piping-hot large black coffee. Maggie smiled, took the cup, and headed for the door.

Just then, Poe hopped down from the window display and rubbed vigorously against her legs. His purr rumbled while he found a square of sunlight. After a languid stretch, he sat as if granting permission for her to continue. Maggie scooped him up, nuzzled his head, and placed him atop a tower of stacked books capped by a treasure chest brimming with volumes. Satisfied, Poe wrapped his tail around himself and stared outside, blinking slowly at passersby.

Just then Joshua entered, smelling faintly of cedar and fresh paint.

"Good morning," he said, looking her up and down. "Wow."

"What?"

"You look really nice," he said.

"Thanks," she answered, cheeks flushing.

"Are you … meeting someone at the book fair?"

Maggie peered over her glasses. "No. Why?"

"Just wondering. You look like you're going on a date."

"It's a date with destiny. I'm hoping to find real

gems, diamonds in the rough at a good price," she said, eyes twinkling.

"Oh, well, that sounds fun. If you're there all day, maybe I'll meet up with you later," Joshua stuttered.

Maggie, too excited to notice his hint, blurted that tickets were likely gone and door prices much higher.

"But try if you want. I need to get in line," she said and slipped outside. Behind the wheel, coffee in the holder, she wondered if she'd missed something Joshua meant.

Nah, she muttered, then drove across town. Her secret parking spot waited. She joined the line. A handful of bookworms stood ahead, reading their own books. Maggie had two books in her bag, along with her pass, trail mix, umbrella and spending cash. The air smelled of damp concrete and the distant spice of street-cart pretzels.

Yet Joshua's words nagged her.

Maybe I'll meet up with you later.

Maybe I'll meet up with you *later?*

Maybe I'll meet up with you later.

Did he really want to meet her? She couldn't focus on her book. Lines blurred like scenery outside a train window.

No. She shook her head to dislodge the thought.

A rumble of distant thunder rolled across the horizon, making a few people in line tuck their paperbacks beneath jackets. Maggie opened her umbrella, silver spokes clicking into place, and offered a quiet nod to the woman behind her, who held a well-loved mystery over her head.

Time breezed by. The clouds thickened, then split with a bright flash, and the doors finally opened. Event staff in maroon polo shirts scanned tickets and passed out canvas totes emblazoned with the fair's fountain-pen logo. Maggie tucked her umbrella under her arm and stepped inside, heart fluttering as the scent of ink swept over her.

Maggie looked behind her and saw the line of people wrapped around the building and down the sidewalk. She smiled. She was among her own kind. She knew this because the other folks around her in line didn't even try to talk to her and kept their noses buried in their books.

Chapter 2

The convention center quickly filled up. The booths ranged from simple folding tables stacked with used books to elaborate displays mimicking bookstores, not unlike the setup of The Bookish Café. Maggie was in her element.

Along the west wall of the convention center were the signing stations of local authors. Along the east wall was the book-cover-designer gallery. Across the central aisle, banners fluttered in the air conditioning. Fluorescent lights reflected off a polished floor, and a tinny public-address system pinged, announcing panel times in a cheerful yet slightly distorted voice.

Maggie strolled down the first aisle, enjoying the

hum of overlapping conversations that flowed around her without them being directed at her. She liked that she knew no one yet felt welcome. Her plan was to loop through the entire hall, note the titles she loved, and decide what she had to have immediately, what could wait for a potential price drop tomorrow, and what might simply add interest to the shelves at the Café, like the handbook on fly-fishing lures she had just spotted.

The overall mood was calm, although employees answered questions from lost attendees and vendors fretted over displays that hadn't arrived or boxes of books that had been damaged in transit. Some attendees took their reading very seriously. One man wore a T-shirt that read "Behave Yourself or You'll End Up in My Novel." Another shirt proclaimed *Carpe Librum*—seize the book. A chalkboard easel boasted the slogan "Eat. Sleep. Read. Repeat." in looping cursive, and a cluster of teens took selfies beneath it, striking dramatic poses with hardcovers held like stage props. Maggie paused to admire a display of enamel pins shaped like tiny open volumes and mentally marked the vendor as a potential supplier.

Maybe Joshua would like one, she mused, then shook her head. It was an intrusive thought. She didn't want to focus on Joshua when she was having so much fun. Thinking about him was pleasant; she simply didn't want to imagine feelings that might not exist. *See how simple that is? Just push it out of your mind,* she told herself, steering toward Authors Row.

Some tables were busier than others. The first to draw a sizable crowd featured a female author. Maggie stretched to see the title of the book, which showed a hulking cowboy clutching a Laura-Ingalls look-alike. *Lust in the Dustbowl* made her chuckle, and she considered buying a signed copy for the bookstore. The author, Serafina Lawson, resembled a romance heroine herself, with wild curly hair and wearing a flowing red dress. She laughed, whispered, laughed again, and thanked each reader with a warm handshake. This was how a visiting writer should behave, enjoying her fans and chatting happily. *Lust in the Dustbowl* wasn't Maggie's cup of tea, but the line said plenty about its popularity.

For a moment Maggie lingered, listening to Serafina tease a blushing reader about "dust storms that heat up more than the sky," sending a ripple of giggles through the queue. Serafina was slated for the evening meet-and-greet. *Alexander would have no trouble striking up a conversation,* Maggie's conscience whispered. That settled it; she would speak to Serafina tonight, if she could get close.

Farther along, a tall, black-clad man had a dozen fans around a table stacked with graphic novels. Maggie rarely read the genre yet stopped anyway. The art, rendered in meticulous cross-hatching, took her breath away. Tiny diagonal lines layered on one another produced shadows so rich that distant cityscapes seemed to float behind the panels. One oversize book she lifted must have taken years to finish. The creator would be at the meet-and-greet, too; she could ask about his process later rather than interrupt now.

"You know what you did!" A loud male voice sliced through the chatter. Conversation froze across Authors Row.

"Look, I'm a writer. I write what I know. If you don't like it, don't read my book. It's as simple as that," said a beanstalk of a man behind a folding table draped with a plain white cloth, stacks of books flanking him.

"You ruined my life!" shouted the other man. He wore a rumpled suit that looked slept in. His tie was crooked. Wild-eyed, he punctuated each word by waving his arms. Maggie wondered whether he had a nose ring before squinting: it was a mole.

"I have the feeling it was ruined before I wrote a single word," the author retorted. Wrong move. The man in the suit swept half the books off the table with one hand, grabbed the author's collar with the other, and nearly dragged him across the tabletop. With clenched teeth inches from the writer's face, he threatened bodily harm.

Maggie and another woman who was also waiting for Serafina Lawson knelt to gather the scattered books. Neither of them took their eyes off the men. Maggie glanced at a cover and recognized the title: *Small Town Secrets* by Otto Deitz. She had stocked it on the new-release shelf, and copies had sold out quickly. What was going on?

"Why, you little smart-aleck! I'll break all your fingers, and you'll never write again!" the man bellowed until two security guards arrived.

Their presence cooled the scene. The suit-clad man released Otto's collar. Otto swatted the hand away, stared him down, and murmured, "Just wait until the sequel comes out."

The man lunged, but security held him. "You're a dead man, Deitz! Do you hear me? I'll get you for this—if it's the last thing I do!"

Otto waved him off, ran a hand through his salt-and-pepper hair, and stepped around the table.

Maggie handed him a stack, and he muttered thanks. The other woman, a thickset attendee with a deep spray tan and dramatically teased hair, returned the remaining books and launched into excited chatter.

"Sorry you had to witness that," Otto said bitterly. He opened a fresh copy, clicked a pen, and asked, "Who should I make this out to?"

Maggie moved on. Authors Row felt too volatile. Otto didn't seem too shaken; perhaps he expected trouble. She decided she would wait for the evening meet-and-greet, where conversation would be easier.

As she rounded the corner into the next aisle, a gentle aroma of roasted coffee beans drifted from a pop-up café stand, mingling with the papery scent of gently used hardcovers. She paused to sip from a water fountain. The day was young, and her list of potential purchases was already growing. Somewhere beyond the next booth, a floor manager barked instructions about restocking mystery titles. Three teens scurried by wearing homemade capes that brushed her ankles. One cape bore hand-painted stars; another glittered with sequins that dropped behind them like breadcrumbs. Maggie smiled, sensing that creativity here was contagious.

Focus, Maggie. Start with the travel section, then circle back to collectibles, she reminded herself. She turned toward a cozy nook strewn with vintage globes and brittle atlases, unaware that Joshua's compliment from that morning was floating back to the front of her thoughts.

Somewhere in the distance, thunder rumbled again, muffled by the vast roof, yet the hall's fluorescent bulbs flickered for half a second. The collective gasp that rose from vendors and visitors alike felt like a shared heartbeat, then conversation resumed, louder than before, as though everyone wanted to prove the storm could not dampen their excitement. Maggie adjusted her glasses, squared her shoulders, and plunged into the maze of shelves, even though the last thing Maggie heard before she disappeared around the corner from Authors Row was still in her head. It was Otto saying, "I had a feeling this might happen."

Chapter 3

After the dust had settled and the book fair returned to normal, Maggie spent the entire day roaming around and left the event with a bag full of sweet bookmarks, name-plates, and a stack of pulp-fiction books from the 1940s that had titles like *Murder Steals the Spotlight* and *The Case of the Haunted Husband*. They would never win prizes for literary genius or be included in any celebrity book club, but Maggie loved them. Their covers were always painted in garish colors. The women were depicted in tight blouses and pencil skirts with pouty lips. The square-jawed men donned fedoras and pin-striped suits, usually holding a gun. They were easy reads that would take Maggie an hour, two at most, to finish between some of the heavier titles she enjoyed. Like people who cue up reruns to relax after work, Maggie grabbed an old piece of pulp fiction that the author had been paid a dollar a page to write. Plus, she loved the old, antique-ish, damp-basement smell these books always had. It was a guilty pleasure she couldn't wait to display at home.

There wasn't a lot of time for her to rearrange her knick-knacks to showcase her new finds. The author meet-and-greet was at eight, and it was already six. She had to freshen up, change her clothes, and get back to her secret parking spot in the span of two hours.

The day had been so much fun that she barely realized how fast time went by. She wasn't even tired as she stepped out of her cottage, carefully watching for Mrs. Peacock, her landlady. If Mrs. Peacock cornered her, she'd get sucked into a conversation about her wealthy landlady not having nearly enough money to survive, her fixed income being so fixed.

Maggie was sure she saw movement by the back door of the main house. She lived in the cottage, also known as a bungalow or mother-in-law house, on Mrs. Peacock's property. She adored the space; it was just enough for her. Besides, her landlord had one of the most beautiful yards in all of Fair Haven. The rivalry between Mrs. Peacock and Mrs. Donovan down the street was as great as the feud between the Hatfields and McCoys. Each year, whether it was a patriotic summer display or the twinkling of hundreds of white lights at Christmas, Maggie could rest assured she lived on the most beautiful property around.

"Margaret? Margaret, can I speak with you for a moment?" Mrs. Peacock called. Where had she been hiding? The old woman was like a ninja. Maggie let out a deep breath and began concocting her escape.

"Hi, Mrs. Peacock. I'm actually on my way to a thing," she said, pointing to her car as if that were explanation enough. It wasn't.

"My dear, I must talk to you. I'm planning on having the driveway to your house redone. I'm sick to death of this gravel. It's just a terrible eyesore. Mr. Peacock—God rest his soul—wanted to do this ages ago, and we just never got around to it. I've managed to scrape up the money, but it leaves me with very little left over. I'm on a fixed income, you know."

"That sounds fine. I'll park on the street," Maggie smiled and pointed again to her car as if it were eagerly waiting for her.

"You'll do no such thing. I won't have my property looking like some street festival. You'll park on the circle drive. Just make sure to pull all the way up so your car will be out of view."

Maggie wasn't sure what one car parked on the street had to do with a festival, but she knew better than to question her landlord. She also knew that her beat-up old Dodge Neon was not the kind of car usually spotted in front of the old girl's main house. Audis and Cadillacs, with the occasional Lexus, were the cars that parked in front of Mrs. Peacock's home.

"Oh, okay. I'll be sure to do that."

"Also, Margaret, since I am having this work done, I need you to make sure that you pay your rent on time. It's what keeps me afloat and out of the poorhouse."

"Yes, ma'am," Maggie replied, biting her tongue. In all the years she'd lived on Mrs. Peacock's property, she had never once been late with rent. Not just because of Mrs. Peacock's insistence that she was dirt-poor and ten dollars away from eating out of garbage cans, but because paying on time was the right thing to do. It annoyed her none-theless, since everyone in town knew Mrs. Peacock was one of the wealthiest people in Fair Haven.

"All right. Now that we've gotten that taken care of, where are you going in such a rush?" Mrs. Peacock folded her arms, her bejeweled fingers and manicured nails sparkling.

"It's a meet-and-greet for the authors at the book fair," Maggie said, squinting through her glasses.

"That does sound lovely. I wonder if Serafina Lawson will be there," Mrs. Peacock mused, making Maggie's face light up.

"Do you know her? She was at the convention signing her book. She was next to Otto—"

"Otto Deitz? Otto Deitz is there? I can't believe he had the audacity to show his face in town. My goodness. At the risk of spreading gossip, I'll just tell you this: stay away from Otto Deitz unless you want your reputation ruined," Mrs. Peacock said before looking at her gold watch. "Oh, would you look at the time. I must get back to the house, my dear. Have fun. Remember to park all the way up on the circle drive." She turned quickly, shuffling up the sidewalk in gold-colored flip-flops that comple-mented the gold stitching in her emerald kaftan.

Although Maggie was stunned that Mrs. Peacock mentioned Otto Deitz, she was even more shocked that her landlady had warned her about him. That was a sure sign she should not only buy his book but seek him out at the meet-and-greet to see what shook loose.

Chapter 4

After parking and smoothing out her skirt, Maggie hurried to the hotel across the street from the convention center where the author meet-and-greet was taking place. The sounds of the town made her feel alive: honking horns, people chatting as they walked past on their way to dinner or a movie or to run a late-evening errand. A motorcycle rumbled to a stop just a few feet ahead, making Maggie wonder how brave the rider had to be to drive at night. The hotel restaurant, a place called G's, had a sign on the door reading "Closed for a Private Party." With her badge ready, she walked in and was greeted by a professional-looking fellow at a long white table with name tags on it.

"Good evening. May I have your name?" the man said without cracking a smile.

"Maggie Bell. Margaret Bell," she answered. Looking over the table, she spotted her name tag. The man checked her name off the list on a clipboard, reached under the table, and gave her a small bag of goodies before he finally smiled.

"Have a good evening, Miss Bell," he said, his smile falling away as quickly as it had popped up. Maggie muttered a quick "Thank you" and headed into the room where the meeting and greeting were well underway.

It was an intimate venue that probably held no more than seventy-five people if crammed in tight. Maggie had been in biker bars and coffee bars. She'd crashed parties and spied on some from a distance. Now she was in a room with not just local authors who had made names for themselves but also the people who read them. Her hands were sweating as she walked farther into the room. She had thought this would be an occasion where people dressed up. The only one dressed fancier than Maggie was Serafina Lawson, who had changed from her red dress to a purple one with matching high heels and a feathery doohickey in her hair. She looked like an old-time saloon gal.

Without hesitating, Maggie walked up to the small crowd around Serafina and caught the tail end of a dirty joke that made the circle burst out laughing. Some slipped away after that; others loitered around her, waiting for another story. But one managed to place himself center stage.

"Fifi, you are too much," he said as Maggie watched him try to slip his arm around her waist. Fifi was having none of it and graciously turned to face him, patted him on the chest, and spoke.

"Of that I am well aware," she smiled, her cheeks displaying two of the most perfect dimples. She looked at Maggie and bounced her eyebrows. "Are you lost, honey? You look like the cat's got your tongue."

"Oh, no ma'am. I just wanted to say hello and that… I just love your outfit," Maggie replied. She didn't know what came over her. Normally she'd be a stuttering mess, standing in the corner with a plastic cup of warm Coke while everyone else mingled and had fun. For some reason she didn't want to be the observer tonight. She wanted to participate, and what better way than to find the loudest mouth and start there.

"Thank you. I know my style isn't for everybody,

but it seems to suit me," she replied with a loud laugh that ended with a slight snort.

The man who had tried to put his arm around her stepped between them. "You look gorgeous, Fifi. You always do."

"Trent, I'm trying to talk to the young lady. Do you mind?" she said; her expression made the man tuck tail and head to the bar, where he ordered something brown in a short glass with ice and tossed it back quickly. "Don't mind him. Just an overly enthusiastic fan. What's your name?"

Maggie introduced herself and, to keep the momentum going, mentioned Mrs. Peacock. "She said to say hello," Maggie lied.

"Vivian Peacock? Oh, my heavens! Do you know we went to high school together? Oh, for the longest time I was so jealous of her. She married the man I loved."

Maggie's eyes nearly popped out of her head. "Really?"

"Well, maybe 'love' is too strong a word. Lust. And maybe it was more his money I was lusting after and not necessarily him," Serafina chortled and snorted again. "A man can look a lot better with a few bucks in his pocket. Am I right?"

Maggie was struck dumb and mesmerized. Dare

she mention this to Mrs. Peacock? *No*—not a word. It would be taken to the grave.

"See, that's the problem with talking to writers. You never know when they are telling the truth or not. But seriously, Vivian Peacock is one of the nicest women I've ever known. How do you know her?"

Maggie explained that Mrs. Peacock was her landlord. She didn't want to detail how wealthy Mrs. Peacock was, so she simply said the property was lovely, safe, and just enough for a single woman like herself to live on.

"If I know Vivian, I'll bet she has the first dollar she ever made framed somewhere in her house. I am going to have to stop by and visit her. Oh, it has been too long," Serafina said, looking off into the distance for a second. For some reason it was easy for Maggie to envision these ladies enjoying each other's company, both wearing brights colors with lots of jewelry, their hair dyed and toenails painted, sitting on Mrs. Peacock's back patio sipping mint juleps. Maggie didn't mind admitting to herself that she'd totally spy and eavesdrop on that visit if the opportunity arose.

Just then Maggie squinted toward the bar and saw Otto Deitz looking right at her. He appeared as serious and sad as he had at the book signing after that angry man slapped all his books off the table. Suddenly her gut tightened. Why was he looking at her like that? Did he think she had something to do with the man acting violent? Surely he couldn't think that.

So why is he staring at me? Maggie wondered, trying to concentrate on what Serafina was saying. Serafina kept talking pleasantly, her eyes darting around the room as she waved and winked at people passing by.

"You sure do have a big following," Maggie said, pulling her gaze away from Otto's.

"When you write erotica, that tends to happen," Serafina giggled.

"I hate to admit I've never read any of your work, but I will pick up a copy tomorrow at the event. I was hoping they might go on sale. After paying for the three-day pass, I'm not ashamed to say I have to watch my pennies," Maggie blurted. Her unease over Otto's stare had triggered nervous babbling.

"I'll do you one better, honey. I've got a couple of copies in my room here at the hotel. I'll grab you one and even sign it." Serafina winked.

"Oh, no. Please don't leave the party on

account of me. Really, Ms. Lawson, it's not necessary. I'm happy to pay for my own copy."

"First, call me Fifi—everybody does. Second, any friend of Vivian Peacock's is a friend of mine. Third, I could use a little break. See that fella at the bar who was getting all handsy just before you walked up?" Maggie knew whom she meant and wrinkled her nose as she blatantly looked right at him. "He's been after me all night. He thinks I've never had a man's attention. Little does he know half my books are based on firsthand experience." Again Maggie's eyes nearly popped out of her skull, making Fifi Lawson laugh.

"Really?"

"See what I mean? You never know when an author is telling the truth. Trent might lose his mind if he knew the truth," Fifi winked and smiled wide, enjoying herself immensely.

"Gosh. Do you want me to call security?" Maggie insisted.

Fifi shook her head. "No. He's harmless."

"If you're sure," Maggie replied. Fifi promised she'd be right back, then left after shaking more hands, giving a few friendly kisses, and assuring several people she'd return in two shakes of a lamb's tail.

Maggie was left standing in the middle of the room while the rest of the crowd mingled. Without thinking she headed toward the bar. She noticed the graphic-novel creator sitting at a table, deep in conversation with some younger fans. She also recognized another author from a book back at the store, but she couldn't recall his name. As far as Maggie knew, he only had one book out. Swamped by people who seemed to be talking more to each other than to him, he didn't appear to say a word. Perhaps she would slip into that group and speak to him later. First, she needed a little courage, so she flagged down the bartender. No one stood between her and Otto Deitz, who was three stools away, when she ordered herself a Shirley Temple.

"A Shirley Temple? I haven't had one of those in years," Otto said. Maggie looked over her glasses at him and squinted.

"I'm not a big drinker," she said bluntly.

"Neither am I," Otto replied and raised his glass, which looked like watered-down scotch. "Cream soda." He pressed a finger to his lips. Maggie smiled.

"I'm Maggie Bell," she said quickly, before the burst of courage from her first sip of the kiddie cocktail could slip away.

"Otto Deitz," he answered, motioning for her to sit next to him.

"How has the book signing been going for you?" she asked.

"Well, it could be better," Otto said, then snapped his fingers. "You were there today. I didn't get a chance to thank you for picking up my books."

"Oh, uh, it was nothing," she replied, pushing her glasses up, but she looked down at her drink. She wanted to ask what that confrontation was all about, yet that wouldn't be polite. Would she want to discuss someone knocking over her books if she were the author?

"I'll bet you're wondering what that was all about," he offered.

She snapped her head up and blinked. "Not if you don't want to talk about it. I would understand,"

"My latest book, well, some folks aren't happy about it. Have you ever read *Peyton Place*? Someone your age might never have heard of it."

"Oh yes, by Grace Metalious. Very scandalous for its day," Maggie replied.

"Well, let's just say Fair Haven has had some scandals revealed, and even though I changed the names, some people aren't happy," Otto said, raising his glass before taking a sip.

Maggie swallowed a gulp of her drink and looked at Otto. "Really?"

"That's what that man was angry about. I know him. Dane McKenny. Of course that isn't his name in the book. I thought I disguised him fairly well, but he gave himself away. Hot-headed." Otto shook his head.

Maggie wasn't sure what to do. She didn't know Dane McKenny or Otto Deitz, and she wasn't certain she wanted to know more. The longer he talked, the more she wished she'd gone to speak with the author whose name eluded her, who remained stoic amid the gabbling crowd.

"Have you read my book?" Otto asked.

"No. I have a list of titles I'm working through. I don't get to many contemporary authors. Lack of time, not interest," It was true she had a long list: titles Mr. Whitfield had written down for her, one of the last things he gave her before he passed away.

"Oh? So what is it that keeps you from reading more contemporary books?" Otto asked, his tone suggesting he didn't believe her.

She straightened her back. "I work at The

Bookish Café. I've been there for years and have read almost every book on the shelves. The previous owner was a collector of old books, classics, first editions, unusual topics. It's quite an eclectic collection. I'm working my way through it. I think I've got about three more shelves to go before I've read almost everything."

"Really? You don't look like the kind of woman who would be interested in old books, classics. I saw you talking with Serafina Lawson. I would have definitely pegged you for a fan of hers."

"Well, I'd think an author would know the old saying 'don't judge a book by its cover,'" Maggie replied. She decided she'd had enough, sucked the last of her Shirley Temple until the straw gurgled at the bottom of the glass, then slid off her barstool.

"Here. In case you get bored with the classics and want to know what your neighbors are up to," Otto pulled a copy of his book from a small plastic shopping bag on the barstool next to him. "Or you can use it to prop up a wobbly chair, whichever comes first. I think I can guess by looking at you."

Maggie took the book and dropped it into her goody bag. She wondered if he'd even signed it. She smiled. "Thank you. I promise to read it."

"Doesn't matter," Otto shrugged.

At that, Maggie let the smile fall right off her face, furrowed her brow, before quickly dropping a dollar on the bar for the bartender. She couldn't tell if he was conceited or simply even more socially inept than she was. It was an impossible call, and she didn't want to stick around to collect any more clues.

"Looks like I've offended another citizen of Fair Haven. I just can't catch a break. I doubt anyone else will talk to me," Otto said, looking rather pleased with himself.

Maggie wished him a good night. Just as she turned away, the other woman who had helped scoop up Otto's books appeared out of nowhere, hair teased even higher than before. As though Maggie weren't there, she looked past her directly at the author. Obviously she wanted to speak to Otto desperately. Maggie was happy to pass the baton. No sooner had she walked off than the woman climbed onto the empty seat beside him.

How could a man who was living what Maggie was sure was a dream existence—writing books for a living—be so surly? He set his own hours; he could work in pajamas if he wanted.

Although that never really appealed to Maggie, she knew plenty of people who thought rolling out of bed and working in flannel pants and a T-shirt was a real perk. Otto didn't have to deal with people and could keep any schedule he liked. Working at night while the world slept, classical music playing, typing by the soft glow of a desk lamp and maybe a crackling fireplace in the background. That sounded perfect.

Peeking over her shoulder, she saw he'd already become engrossed in conversation with the lady who had waited for an opening. *Groupies are everywhere,* Maggie thought. She suspected the woman had more on her mind than an autographed copy of *Small-Town Secrets.*

When Maggie turned around, she was immediately flagged down by Fifi, who elbowed into the crowd surrounding the other author and pulled him away by the hand. The crowd followed like ducks in a row.

"Have you met Mr. Thomas James?" Fifi gushed.

Maggie shook her head, pushed up her glasses, and extended her hand. Her heart raced; being thrust at people was not her comfort zone, but Fifi wasn't the sort who took *no* for an answer, though she'd given *no* to Trent at least three times for what-ever he kept whispering in her ear.

Maggie saw a twitch at the corner of Mr. James's lips that she assumed was a smile. No one could orbit Fifi and stay stone-faced for long.

"He's written several wonderful books on Fair Haven, being born and raised here. Who would have believed there were so many interesting facts about this little town?" Fifi exclaimed, elbowing Trent's arm away from her waist.

"Oh, have you compared notes with Mr. Deitz?" Maggie asked innocently. Mr. James's slight smile vanished and migrated to the corner of his left eye.

"No," was all Mr. James said.

Fifi burst out laughing, as did half the crowd. Maggie felt an icy grip around her heart; her cheeks flushed.

"You'd have no way to know, my dear. Those two don't get along—*at all*," Fifi explained.

"Did he write about you in his book too?" Maggie hadn't meant to blurt that, but it struck a bull's-eye.

"I'm not concerned with the drivel he's scrib-bled in his 'novel.' I'm a historian, not a gossip columnist," Mr. James air-quoted, staring into the distance like Christopher Lee in, well, any film he'd ever starred in. Maggie couldn't help liking the response; she smiled, glanced at her shoes for a second, then looked up. Without moving his head, Mr. James looked down at her, arched his right eyebrow, and twitched the corner of his lip. A smile, or the closest he could manage.

"Always so serious," Fifi chuckled, pulling Maggie aside to give her the signed copy she'd promised.

Though Maggie doubted she'd enjoy such a racy novel, she accepted graciously. She fetched another Shirley Temple and quietly made her way to each author. Some had brought copies of their books, and Maggie bought one from each—how rude would it have been not to? Delicious hors d'oeuvres circulated. Conversations grew louder and more animated as the evening wore on, even though Maggie, still fighting shyness, stayed on the periphery. She listened, watched with fascination, and, when addressed, managed to contribute an opinion or two.

The hours flew by. Before Maggie realized the time, the event was ending. She wanted to say good night to Fifi and Mr. James, who had been stoic like The Thinker all evening, becoming more comical by the hour. But neither was there. With her goody bag and sack of newly signed books, Maggie was first to head toward the door.

A scream stopped her. Not a startled squeak over a spilled drink. This was a scream unlike any other. Someone was desperate and terrified.

Chapter 5

Maggie dashed out of the restaurant and into the lobby of the hotel. It was eerily quiet; no employee stood at the front desk and no guest lounged in the seating area, except for Fifi, who staggered from the elevator bank with her arm draped over her eyes.

Trent appeared out of nowhere and nearly knocked Maggie to the ground as he raced to catch Fifi in his arms. Before she could stop herself, Maggie shuffled past the distraught woman, who proceeded to gasp into Trent's chest, much to his delight.

Carefully she peeked around the corner. Nothing lay ahead but an elevator whose doors bounced repeatedly against a foot that blocked them from closing. That foot belonged to Otto Deitz. He was lying on the floor, his head at an awkward angle, his eyes closed. Blood seemed to seep from the back of his head, and red marks ringed his neck.

Maggie pulled back and looked at the crowd quickly forming at the restaurant door. Fifi was crying. Trent consoled her. The professional greeter who had taken Maggie's name earlier appeared. As Maggie backed out of the elevator bank, the man ran past her, looked inside at the still-bouncing door, then clapped a hand over his mouth. Without a word he spoke into a walkie-talkie while hurrying back to the phone by the front desk. One call summoned the manager on duty to the elevators; the other went to 911.

Maggie glanced at the gathering guests and wondered who could have done this. Was the guilty person still among the book-fair attendees who, like her, had simply hoped to chat with authors and gather stories for work the next day? This was going to be one heck of a story to tell.

Within minutes police officers, an ambulance crew, and a woman in a black suit arrived. Thankfully, Officer Gary Brookes was among the cops assigned to the scene. As soon as he saw Maggie, he hurried to her side.

"What the heck is going on?" he asked quietly while other officers took statements and EMTs confirmed there were no signs of life from Mr. Deitz.

"Do you want the facts, or the facts as I see them?" Maggie asked. Gary had known her since high school; they had always been friends. The only difference now was that Gary had grown taller, built more muscle, and looked very handsome in uniform.

"How do you see them?" he asked, knowing Maggie's eye for detail.

"Well, I think you're going to have a hard time whittling down the suspect list," she said, then launched into the tale of Otto Deitz and his tell-all book about the "seedy underbelly" of Fair Haven.

"Did you really just say *seedy underbelly*?" Gary shook his head.

"Well, that's what it sounds like he wrote. I've got a copy in my goody bag that he gave me."

Maggie told him what she knew so far. He took out his notepad and started writing Maggie's statement.

"Stay here, and I'll give you a lift when I'm done," Gary said, expressionless.

"My car is parked outside. I can drive myself."

"No. Wait for me. Make yourself comfortable; I'll walk you to your car," he practically whispered, and Maggie noticed.

"Why are we whispering?"

"Private investigator," Gary murmured, jerking his chin toward the woman in the suit.

"Really? I thought P.I.s were only used for nasty divorces and workers' compensation fraud," Maggie said.

"Maybe that's what's happening," Gary shrugged. "All I know is she arrived this morning and has been following Otto Deitz on his signing tour. He had two stops prior to this, and there have been death threats at each one. Can you believe that—death threats for writing a book?"

Maggie's heart jumped. She couldn't wait to get home and read it. Considering the chaos in the hotel lobby, she suspected it was going to be a long night.

While Gary helped other officers take statements, cordon off the elevator bank, and usher the crime-scene photographer in to snap away, Maggie lingered near the front desk where a wall-mounted monitor displayed the hotel's CCTV feeds. Most cameras showed nothing but dim corridors and closed doors—until she saw movement in one frame. Two men were trying to exit through the pool area.

She glanced across the lobby and spotted the sign that pointed one way to the workout room and the other way to the swimming pool. With everyone's attention fixed on the elevator, no one noticed her slip down the side hall.

Only the floodlights glowed inside the pool enclosure, and the water lay perfectly still, catching the pale under-lighting like a sheet of glass. The atmosphere felt uncanny, the kind of hush that makes a person whisper even when no one else is present.

Maggie peeked in and saw the men standing beneath the red EXIT sign. The door had one of those horizontal crash bars striped yellow and red, warning that an alarm would sound if it were pushed. The pair appeared to be arguing over whether to risk it.

Maggie hesitated. Should she fetch Gary? If she did, they might slip away, or trigger the alarm and vanish into the night. Yet confronting two possibly dangerous men alone could turn into a hostage situation. *Or,* she reasoned, *they could be harmless guests who forgot swimsuits and wore black hoodies to the pool for some unfathomable reason.*

Her thoughts tangled until the larger man shouted, "We have to do something!" The outburst made Maggie jump and rattle the door handle. Both figures snapped their heads toward her. Their hoods cast dark shadows where eyes should have been, but she felt their stare. The bigger man took two steps in her direction. That was enough for Maggie's fight-or-flight response to pick *flight*.

In dress shoes with the slightest kitten heels, she lurched down the hall, half running, half hobbling, like someone trying to sprint across a balance beam. In her mind she might as well have been wearing stilettos on wet cement.

Back in the lobby, nearly all the guests had dispersed. The hotel's night shift employees were standing around, whispering and gawking while the police finished up their interviews.

"Ahem!" Maggie cleared her throat. Gary looked up from his notes, which he was sharing with the woman in the dark suit, the private investigator.

"You need something, darlin'?" the woman asked. Her icy-blue eyes and unsmiling lips reminded Maggie of Thomas James's perpetual stone face.

"I … uh … Officer Brookes, please. There are people in the pool area, and I think they're trying to leave unnoticed," Maggie said, gesturing over her shoulder.

At that moment, a siren shrieked as the pool-door alarm activated. Apparently the men had decided to take their chance.

Gary bolted toward the pool. The P.I. scowled at Maggie, drew a yellow stun gun from a side holster beneath her jacket, and strode out the front entrance. Some of the hotel staff, a maid and a front desk clerk, gasped at the sight of the stun-gun and huddled together.

Maggie wanted to follow Gary, but the investigator's frosty glare rooted her in place. After a tense few minutes, Gary returned alone. The P.I. shot him a questioning look; he shook his head. No arrests.

"Well, would you like to tell me your name and explain why you waited to mention two suspicious characters loitering by the pool?" the P.I. snapped. Her anger was clearly aimed at Maggie.

"Agnes Krueger, this is Maggie Bell," Gary

interjected. "We've known each other since high school. I'm sure she—"

"You might have cost me the apprehension of a killer, Miss Bell. What do you have to say to that?" Agnes demanded.

"Maybe you should have been investigating instead of interviewing like a police officer," Maggie blurted, blinking innocently. Gary rolled his eyes so far back that Maggie feared he saw his own brain. She hadn't meant to be rude; blunt honesty was her default, or so she told herself. Agnes Krueger did not look convinced.

"Are you trying to tell me how to do my job?" Agnes asked, staring her down. She was a traditionally pretty woman with curves in all the right places, but the fine lines around her eyes suggested a past that allowed no nonsense now.

"No ma'am," Maggie said, swallowing.

"Then get her out of here."

"I'm going," Maggie huffed. Gary guided her toward the exit.

"Don't skip town," he murmured, ushering her into the revolving door. "I'll call you later. Hey, Dutch, walk Maggie to her car, would you?"

Dutch was one of the uniformed officers on the

scene. He nodded, but Maggie put up her hand and shook her head. "I'll be fine. Talk to you later."

She clutched her goody bag and purse tight to her chest. She didn't dare say anything else while Agnes Krueger glared. Did that woman really think Maggie had something to do with Otto Deitz's death? He was at least six inches taller and outweighed her by fifty pounds; there was no way she could have inflicted that kind of damage.

It was after ten o'clock, and most of Fair Haven had turned in for the night. All the businesses were closed, and the main drag was devoid of cars. Maggie quietly made her way to her special parking spot and smiled at the sight of her old jalopy patiently waiting. She unlocked the driver's door, slid inside, pulled the door shut, and locked it. For a moment she sat in the darkness, taking slow breaths. If Otto's book was as juicy as he'd hinted, half the town could be suspects. Yet why would he receive death threats on a regional book tour? Who in a big city would care about local gossip from Fair Haven?

"I guess it depends on what he wrote," Maggie muttered, rolling down her window. Her Dodge Neon must be one of the last cars with manual locks and cranks; the cool night air helped clear her head.

She began rummaging through her goody bag for *Small Town Secrets* but froze before rolling the window up. A metallic bang—someone had toppled a trash can—and shuffling footsteps. Maggie ducked low in her seat.

"We didn't do anything, okay? You need to calm down," a hushed voice said.

Peeking over the dash, Maggie saw two people whose builds matched the pair from the pool, though they now wore different clothes. She held her breath.

"But we didn't say anything either. What if someone saw us? Maybe we should have stayed to help. My mom will—"

Mom? Maggie thought. Hard to see in the darkness, but the voices sounded late-teen, early-twenties. The taller one bounced nervously from right foot to left.

"Your mom will be thankful you didn't get caught and thrown in jail. Look, we didn't do anything. As far as we know, it was like that when we got there, and we just left. Simple," the smaller one said. They exhaled together, then turned toward Maggie's car. She kept still.

"Why is there a car there?" the big one asked.

"Because it's a parking spot. I don't know," the smaller replied.

"Let's check it out."

"It's a beater. Nothing worth money in there."

"How do you know?"

Maggie's mind raced. Even locked in, they'd spot her through the open window. Desperate, she sat upright, twisted the key, and flicked on her high beams. Blinding light flooded the alley. The two figures flung arms over their faces, cursed, and bolted the way they'd come.

Heart hammering, Maggie started the engine, pulled away, and headed home. She'd tell Gary everything in the morning; tonight had delivered more than enough excitement.

All the way home she rehearsed a description of the two men. Reaching her block, she remembered to park on Mrs. Peacock's circle drive, out of neighbors' view. She cut the engine and listened: no voices, no strange headlights, just the porch glow and solar path lights. With her house key ready, she grabbed her haul, trotted along the path, unlocked her door, slipped inside, and snapped the deadbolt.

Within minutes she was in pajamas, sipping hot tea, butter cookies on a plate, and *Small Town Secrets* open before her. Otto had signed it, an illegible scrawl. She read deep into the night until a knock at six a.m. jolted her.

It was Gary.

"Have I got news for you," he said, stepping inside.

"Oh yeah? Well, I've got news for *you*," Maggie replied, scratching her head. She'd never slept; only two pages remained in Otto's book. She waved the paperback at him.

"Before you start, please tell me you have coffee," Gary said.

Maggie nodded, eyes widening as though he'd voiced the world's best idea. "Yes. I could use a cup myself. I finished my tea and cookies. Gary, brace yourself for the biggest suspect pool you've ever faced. Otto's book points fingers at several people I actually know. According to him, there's a scandal behind almost every door in town."

"It can't be that bad," he yawned.

"Give me a minute," Maggie said, dumping extra scoops of grounds into the filter. "You wouldn't believe what I read. Fifi Lawson was right. Otto Deitz was a writer, and you never knew when he was telling the truth. Or was."

"Who's Fifi?"

"Serafina Lawson."

Gary shrugged.

"The author who looked like she stepped off an episode of *Real Housewives*," Maggie clarified, raising a brow.

"Oh, that one. Dutch interviewed her. She's a character—distraught, dramatic. I suspect some of it's to sell books."

"Could be, but I'm telling you her steamy novels couldn't hold a candle to the things going on in broad daylight in Fair Haven."

"This sleepy town? The most we handle at the station is an occasional trespassing, maybe some drunk-and-disorderly," Gary said, taking a seat at the kitchen table. He sipped his coffee, then reached for the sugar bowl in the center.

"Right, and then there are those pesky murders that crop up every once in a while," Maggie added.

"All right, Sherlock Holmes. I've got an offer for you." Gary leaned forward, arms folded across his chest. "You tell me what you've found, and I might take you along to question a person of interest."

Maggie stared. "Seriously?"

"If you have something to wash this coffee down with."

Maggie leapt up, yanked open the fridge, and pulled out the raspberry coffee cake she'd been saving for the last day of vacation.

"Wow. I wasn't expecting this," Gary joked, prying open the plastic lid. Maggie handed him a knife and set out two small plates. No way was he eating alone.

After a first forkful, she told Gary everything in the book she thought relevant, especially the passage describing a man conducting a torrid affair under his wife's nose *and* under the nose of his mistress's husband, who also happened to be the cheater's employer.

"Hold on. My brain needs a second. He's having an affair with his boss's wife? That's what you're saying?" Gary asked between bites.

Maggie nodded, hurriedly chewing. "The guy's description fits the man who knocked Otto's books off the table yesterday."

"What did he look like?"

"Big guy, starting to bald." She waved a hand over her crown. "Eyes close together. Suit looked like he slept in it, wrinkled. And he had a mole on the side of his nose."

"Perfect," Gary said with a smirk.

"Why is that perfect?"

"Another witness said the same thing. Suit, mole, bad attitude."

"Do you know who it is?" Maggie asked, downing another bite of cake.

"Yes. I know exactly who he is."

"So do I, but only because he's described *perfectly* in this book, mole and all," Maggie replied, sliding *Small Town Secrets* across the table.

Gary flipped it open, took a sip of coffee, and asked to borrow it. Maggie nodded.

"How about Serafina? She deserves a book of her own. Professional jealousy maybe?" Gary tapped the side of his nose. "She's the one who reported Mr. Mole's tantrum. You ever read her stuff?"

"I don't usually read that genre, though she gave me a copy," Maggie admitted, blushing.

Gary yawned, stretching his arms overhead. "Okay, Miss Bell, I'm going home for a shower and forty winks. I'll pick you up later to talk to our friend. Remember, *I'm* asking the questions; you're just tagging along."

"Fine. I'll nap, too. I still want to get back to the fair. I paid for the whole weekend," Maggie said, stifling her own yawn.

"Even better. What time does it close today?"

"Six," she answered, rubbing her eyes. Food in her stomach made the caffeine useless; fatigue swept in.

"Meet me at the convention center entrance at six. I don't want to confront him at his job. He's had enough bad press. He's not a suspect, only a person of interest."

Maggie gave a thumbs-up while escorting Gary to the door.

"Can you believe after all these years we're still friends?" Gary asked as the morning air hit them.

"What do you mean?"

"I'm comfortable enough to show up unshaven and probably smelling like an all-nighter. You're comfortable enough with smeared makeup and coffee breath. We're a good team," he said, leaning in to kiss the top of her head. "I'll see you at six, and I promise to smell better."

Mortified, Maggie shut the door and hurried to the bathroom mirror. Yup. Mascara smudged like a raccoon, hair flat on one side, sleep crusties in her eyes. *And coffee breath,* she groaned.

After washing her face, she decided on a quick nap. She set her alarm for nine and crawled into bed. Her heart jolted; she'd forgotten to tell Gary about the two suspicious figures at the pool. *That's what happens when you burn the candle at both ends,* she scolded herself. She'd remember tonight.

She fell asleep instantly, and woke five minutes before the alarm buzzed.

Chapter 6

The second day of the book fair was buzzing with excitement and morbid curiosity, as news of the murder had spread across Fair Haven like germs in a kindergarten classroom. Maggie overheard several conversations about how Otto Deitz had died, each one more sensational than the last. There was also a cornucopia of opinions on whether the man had deserved it.

"Hey, when you write a book that bad-mouths everyone in your hometown, you can expect to get a punch in the face," one sci-fi book vendor said.

"A punch in the face, maybe. Murdered? Whatever happened to free speech?" a man buying a couple books from him retorted.

"Is gossip covered under free speech?" asked a woman in a T-shirt that read, *I just want to read books and pet my cat.*

"His book was listed as a novel. People can believe whatever they want. It still isn't an excuse to kill the guy," the buyer replied.

"But he didn't even try to cover up who he was writing about. He may as well have just used their real names and given their addresses too," the vendor countered.

Maggie pushed her glasses up on her nose. She could have stepped in and given her own opinion, but decided not to. She wasn't going to change anyone's mind just because she had seen Mr. Mole knock all the books off Otto's table, or because she'd actually gotten a good look at Mr. Deitz's bloodied body in the elevator.

No. It was best to just keep moving and see if there was anything she might want to buy. She visited some of the booths she'd missed the day before. There were a few publishers who specialized in non-mainstream titles by unknown authors that Maggie found especially interesting. She picked up a few books that she'd read first, then decide if any should be ordered for the bookstore. Although she was biased—she despised the mainstream bestsellers lists—her judgments had loosened since Joshua forced the store to stock more contemporary and popular books. It was nice to see more people reading and have the shop be profitable for once. The descriptions on the backs of a few books sounded like fun, the prices were right, so into her shopping bag they went.

When she looked at her watch, it was already almost four o'clock. Her stomach growled. The slice of coffee cake had long since dissolved in her gut. She was running on empty and needed something to recharge her battery if she was going to keep up with Gary that evening.

The food court was crowded, but the smell of gooey, greasy pepperoni pizza was enough to convince Maggie that standing in line would be worth it. Finally, after only about ten minutes, she had two slices and a large Coke in her hands. She found a quiet corner to sit down and people-watch for a while. The pizza tasted delicious, and the Coke was refreshing. She dug in her bag and looked at her treasures, reading the first paragraphs of each to help her decide which she'd read first. For a few minutes, she almost forgot that a local author had been murdered.

But she was quickly slapped back into that

reality when she looked up and saw the two men from the night before.

Calm down, Mags. Are you sure it's them? You had maybe three hours of sleep. Four at most, she was sure. However, as she started to pack up her books and follow them through the crowd, she saw something even stranger: they were already being followed by Agnes Krueger, the private investigator. The woman who had shown up last night at the hotel in a suit with a stun-gun and read Maggie the riot act for possibly letting a killer slip away.

Swallowing hard, Maggie decided to tail all of them. With her bags slung over her shoulder, she was grateful she'd chosen jeans and gym shoes. Not only could she keep up, but she could stay quiet. Even though they were moving so quickly that Maggie kept bumping into people, tables, and a display or two, she pressed forward. She watched as Agnes Krueger paused and loitered at a display while the two men stood in front of an employee-only door, as if trying to decide whether to stay or go.

They decided to go. Agnes Krueger followed. Maggie kept pace but hesitated before opening the door. Employee-only doors usually led down long, fluorescent-lit hallways with very few places to hide.

So? If you open the door and they're all standing there looking at you, just say oops and leave.

It wasn't against the law to go down an employee-only corridor. It was just frowned upon, her inner voice reasoned. Funny how that little voice always knew how to boost her confidence when it came to getting into trouble, but turned tail and disappeared when dealing with members of the opposite sex.

She took a deep breath and hurried up to the door. A glance over her shoulder confirmed no one was paying attention to her. After one more breath, she turned the latch, yanked the door open, and saw—nothing. She stepped inside and quietly closed the door behind her. For a second she held her breath and listened. At that moment, the loud click of another door closing echoed down the desolate hallway.

She let her breath out and tiptoed, literally, making barely any noise. But since the hallway was long with a high ceiling and solid concrete walls, every tiny sound echoed like the bells of Notre Dame. At least, that was how Maggie heard it.

The corridor was gray from top to bottom, with a couple of thick, random pipes protruding from the floor and merging with the wall. There was a stack of WET FLOOR sandwich boards and another pile of orange safety cones tucked into a corner. There were no doors or cubbies to duck into. It was at least ten degrees cooler in the corridor, and the air smelled strongly of paint and bleach.

Maggie pushed her glasses up on her nose and clung to the wall as she continued slowly down the corridor. Once she reached the end, she peeked around the corner. Not only was she completely alone, but there was nothing there except a fire extinguisher and a heavy exit door.

Thankfully, there were no yellow and red stripes on it to indicate the bar was rigged to an alarm. However, it was a heavy metal door. She pressed her ear to it and tried to listen for anyone who might be just outside. She couldn't hear anything.

She had two choices: either turn around and go back to the book fair or push open this door and see what was happening on the other side.

There was no reason to stand there and dilly-dally. Maggie pushed the door wide open, stepped out into the bright sunshine, took a couple steps, and the door slammed shut behind her. When she turned around, she saw there was no handle. Now she was locked out.

Worse than that, there wasn't anyone around. Where had they gone? Had she really wasted enough time sneaking down the hallway to let everyone get away from her? She took a few steps and realized she'd ended up just a few paces from the special place she'd been parking her car. In an effort to make the whole tail worth her while, Maggie decided to put her bags in the trunk and free up her hands to walk all the way around the building and go in through the front door. However, that was going to prove to be an ordeal. As she approached her car, a very stern, clear female voice ordered her to freeze.

"Don't you move," it said.

Maggie recognized the voice. It was Agnes Krueger. She sounded angry. Swallowing hard, Maggie raised her hands in the air. Her bags, which had been looped over her forearms, fell clumsily to the crooks of her elbows, pulling her into the stance of a scarecrow.

"Turn around. Slowly," she ordered.

"I was just going to put my bags in my car," Maggie said, her eyebrows arched as her glasses slipped to the edge of her nose. When she turned around, she saw Agnes Krueger had her stun-gun aimed right at her. The rush of adrenaline forced her spine to straighten. Her arms went up an inch higher. She tilted her head back to see through her glasses.

"Pretty convenient that your car is here and two suspicious characters I was following made their way directly to it," Agnes Krueger said.

"Uh, yeah?" Maggie didn't know what else to say. Pins and needles started to prick at her shoulders. "Can I set my bags down?"

Agnes Krueger squinted at Maggie. "Slow. Don't make any sudden moves or I'll..."

"I won't," Maggie said, and as slowly as she could, she lowered her bags to the ground, leaving her hands open and fingers splayed while pulling them free from the plastic loops.

Finally free from the weight, Maggie kept her hands up in clear view so Agnes Krueger wouldn't have any reason to freak out. However, inside, Maggie was having a breakdown of her own. She'd been in some tough situations, but having a weapon pointed at her by an angry private investigator had to rank up there with one of the most unnerving.

As if reading her mind, Agnes Krueger lowered her weapon and holstered it beneath her blazer. She looked Maggie up and down.

"You want to tell me what you're doing out here?"

"Like I said," Maggie pushed her glasses up with her thumb, her hands still raised and fingers spread. "I just wanted to put my bags in my car. And... I saw the two guys who had been at the pool last night. So I thought I'd follow them, but you were already doing that, so I thought it would be a good idea to put my things in my car. It doesn't seem like such a good idea now."

"You were following me following them?"

"Yes."

"Any idea where they might have gone? You can put your arms down now."

"No, ma'am."

"I find it very interesting that the guys you saw last night are here today. *You're* here today. They sneak out and just happen to be where you parked your car. How come you didn't park in the garage like the rest of the convention attendees?" Agnes Krueger's eyes never stopped scanning the area, except to bore into Maggie's.

"It's too expensive. No one parks over here even though it's completely legal. I didn't think anything of it. I didn't know an author was going to get killed by some angry people he wrote about in his book.

Have you looked at Otto Deitz's book? You'll find your man in there. Or woman. He wrote about everybody."

"Miss Bell, I've made a career out of studying human behavior. I'm starting to see a pattern in yours."

"A pattern?" Maggie said. Who did this woman think she was? Agnes Krueger didn't know anything about Margaret Bell. She didn't know Maggie still missed her boss, who had been the kindest, gentlest person she'd ever known. She didn't know that Maggie had suffered from severe shyness and was socially awkward almost all the time until...

Until Joshua took over the bookstore.

There was that inner voice trying to get her riled up again. Wasn't it that same voice that told her to go down the corridor and got her into this predicament to begin with?

"Yes. You've got that babe-in-the-woods persona. You might have Officer Brookes on the hook, but let's be honest, we're all girls here. You can rumble with the best of them if your back is against the wall." Agnes Krueger smirked.

"Yeah, well, that doesn't change the fact that you need to read *Small Town Secrets* if you want to find the person who killed Otto Deitz," Maggie replied bluntly. She didn't know why this woman had such a chip on her shoulder, but it was obvious there was no arguing with her. Not at this point.

"I'll be keeping an eye on you, Miss Bell. And in case you think you can hoodwink Officer Brookes into anything risky, I'll be keeping an eye on him, too. My sixth sense is telling me I'm looking at a lot more than meets the eye."

"You're not even from here," Maggie muttered before Agnes glared at her.

"What did you say?"

"Nothing. Stay safe," Maggie blinked without any expression on her face.

"Yeah, yeah. You too," Agnes said, looking Maggie up and down before leaving. With those last words, the P.I. made her way to the sidewalk and headed toward the main entrance of the event center, as Maggie had planned to do. She felt like she'd just been robbed and then dragged behind a car for a few miles.

Was she really a suspect now? Did Agnes really think Maggie could kill someone? What could she possibly believe was the motive? Maggie wanted to tell Gary all about it but then stopped in her tracks. The last thing she would do was put him in any danger. It was one thing for Maggie to take risks by herself. It was another thing entirely to drag her oldest and dearest friend into something that could be detrimental to his career. Agnes Krueger, Private Investigator, was a woman with an ax to grind, and she was going to use anyone as the stone.

With a heavy heart, Maggie hoisted up her bags and made her way to the car. She unlocked it, threw her things in the back, and slammed the hatch shut.

Just then, she heard something scuffling at her feet. When she looked down, she saw a foot that was not her own sticking out from beneath the bumper.

Chapter 7

With a yelp, Maggie jumped back, squatted down, and peered under her car. There wasn't just one pair of shoes, but two. Both were attached to the two people she'd seen at the pool, by her car the night before, and just now being tailed by Agnes Krueger. If Maggie had had the chance, she'd have hidden from Agnes as well.

"Hey! What the heck is going on under there?" she hissed.

"Don't call her back. We surrender," the big one said.

"Shut up! We don't surrender. We didn't do anything, remember!" the little one said, giving his buddy a shove as best he could in such close quarters.

"I saw you guys at the hotel. You killed Otto Deitz, and I'm calling the cops," Maggie quickly backed up and darted in the direction Agnes Krueger had gone. Both young men scrambled out from under the car.

"No! Wait!" the big one whined. "We didn't kill anyone. We aren't killers."

Maggie stopped at the corner of the building. She wouldn't have to run far or fast to reach the main entrance if these two bolted after her. One long, loud scream would be enough to draw attention from the folks milling around the grounds.

"Then what were you doing sneaking out of the hotel? And how come you snuck out by the pool? And what were you doing over here? I saw you by my car that night. It doesn't look good for you two, I'm just saying," Maggie said, squinting as she posed, ready to run.

"It's nothing like that," the little one finally said. "My name is Crush. This is Handy. Can you be trusted? I mean, if we tell you something, can we trust you won't go get that woman?"

"Why would you worry about that if you didn't do anything wrong?" Maggie asked as Handy shifted nervously with his hands in his pockets and Crush tried to look innocent by lowering his chin and looking up at her.

"A woman just asked us to let her know when another guy was going into his room," said Crush. "So, we did. We didn't have anything to do with what happened to him. See, we work at the hotel."

"Bellboys," Handy added.

"Yeah. We work mostly for tips. So, when a woman offered us each a hundred dollars to tip her off when the man was on his way to his room, we did it. We thought it was some kind of romantic thing. Like she was going to surprise him."

"You didn't look like you were on duty," Maggie pressed, looking down her glasses at them. Her muscles had relaxed, as they made no attempt to charge her. Plus, neither one could have been more than twenty-one years old. Just kids who'd found themselves in a bad situation.

"We'd just gotten off and had changed our clothes. Those jackets they make us wear are not all that comfortable," Handy replied with a grimace.

"So, who was the woman who asked you to spy for her? Was she a guest at the hotel? What room did she stay in? Was there anyone with her?" Maggie wanted to get to the bottom of this quickly and Agnes Krueger could head back to wherever she'd come from.

"We don't know. She caught us outside the hotel and said to call her. That's all we did," Crush said, his eyes wide and innocent.

Handy looked down at the ground and kicked a stone. "That's not totally all."

Crush looked up at his sidekick and gave him an elbow to the gut.

"Hey, you don't have to tell me anything more. You can tell Agnes Krueger or the cops or a judge or the other guys in the holding cell with you or..." Maggie squinted and frowned.

"We found a wallet on the ground. It was the guy in the hotel room we were supposed to be watching. We, well, we took the money. But that's all. We didn't take anything else. In fact, we just dropped it and split the cash. But when we came toward the lobby, we saw all the cops and people crying and you spotted us by the pool. We freaked out. That's all."

"And you stole money from a dead guy," Maggie added.

"We didn't know he was dead when we took it," Handy pleaded.

Maggie stood there for a second, letting that

comment sink in. She was over a decade older than these two guys and could remember herself being young and stupid. Maybe not this stupid, but stupid nonetheless. She could give their names to Agnes Krueger and they'd surely lose their jobs. They didn't fit the modus operandi of killers. Not that Maggie was an expert. Agnes Krueger wasn't an expert either. Gary was. And Maggie was an expert at common sense, if she didn't say so herself. Using common sense, it led her to believe Crush and Handy didn't do anything more than what they admitted to. Still, they might be able to help, since a mysterious person had asked them to keep an eye on Otto Deitz.

Who was that woman?

"Look, I don't think the police will come down hard on you. Especially if you go and tell them what you know. Ask for Officer Gary Brookes. He's a friend of mine. Tell him you spoke to me, and he'll help you. That I can promise," Maggie took a deep breath, puffing herself up to be tougher than she really was. "If you don't, I'll tell him myself and you guys can take your chances."

Crush and Handy looked at each other, and there was more than a hint of humanity in their expressions. Just to make it more clear, Maggie added that they might not know it, but they could have information that leads to an arrest. Their names would be in the papers, and they'd be heroes.

"Girls like heroes," Maggie added.

She wasn't sure where that comment came from. It wasn't like her to talk that way. However, they did respond the way she'd hoped. After a couple of mumbled words between the two of them, they agreed.

"Again, it's Officer Gary Brookes. I'll be talking to him tonight. I think the sooner you speak to him, the better," Maggie added.

Crush and Handy nodded, and before Maggie could say anything more, they were on their way in the opposite direction of the convention center. She took a deep breath and turned to go back into the book fair.

Chapter 8

When six o'clock finally rolled around, Maggie stood at the curb, scanning the road for Gary's squad car. One thing about him: he was always punctual. She saw him pull up in front of the convention center and park. All afternoon, she'd debated whether to meet Gary as planned and risk Agnes Krueger seeing them or go M.I.A. and dig up clues on her own. She decided that a private investigator couldn't damage a police officer's career unless they caught him doing something illegal. Going to talk to a suspect was not illegal.

Maggie wasn't going to be scared off by Agnes. Especially when Fair Haven was her town. Strangers were welcome, but don't start stirring the pot like you run the kitchen. When Maggie finally emerged from the convention center's front doors, she scanned the area for Agnes hiding in a car or peeking out from behind a tree or mailbox. She didn't see anything, but that didn't mean no one was watching. The sun instantly warmed her skin, chilled by the air conditioning inside. Maggie marched right up to the squad car.

"Do I need to ride in back?" Maggie asked through the open passenger side window.

"Not until you break the law. You've come close, but so far, not yet," Gary teased.

She climbed in, and Gary told her what he'd found out.

"Turns out the characters in the book, Zane McGinny and Lisa Forhee, are pseudonyms for Dane McKenny and Lora Foretree. Talk about doing the bare minimum to conceal the identities of the guilty," Gary said, shaking his head.

"How did you find this out?"

"It wasn't hard. I spoke with your landlady. She'd read the book and was absolutely mortified," Gary said. This proved what a good policeman Gary really was. Other cops might have put out APBs looking for someone who matched descriptions in the book. He could have rounded up the usual suspects of vandals and petty thieves to ask if they'd heard anything on the street. Instead, he went to the most reliable source in town: one of Fair Haven's most robust grapevines, Mrs. Vivian Peacock. If she didn't know who the author was referring to, no one would.

"What was she mortified about? She wasn't in the book," Maggie replied.

"Exactly. She called the author a hack. How could he write about such cliché issues when there were perfectly good stories all around town, like how her garden was the prize jewel of Fair Haven and how her husband, God rest his soul, gave so much to his community while at the same time being a saintly and attentive husband." Gary laughed.

"That sounds like Mrs. Peacock all right." Maggie laughed too.

"Yes. But she gave me the similar-sounding names. Dane McKenny fits the description Serafina Lawson gave of the man who knocked all the books off Otto's table yesterday."

Maggie tapped her chin. "Yes. I've only seen Dane a couple of times. He's a lawyer, isn't he? Men who wear suits make me nervous. Especially when they're mussed-up suits."

"No. He runs a meat locker and supplies to a few places. The guy makes a pretty penny. People will pay for good meat. Not to mention he gets some exotic stuff like ostrich and alligator," Gary replied.

Maggie did a double take. "You're kidding me," she said, squinting and looking down her glasses at him.

"No, I'm not."

"Have you ever eaten ostrich or alligator?" Maggie asked.

"No. But I guess some people like it. I've heard alligator can be good. Let's put it this way: if I were really, really hungry, I'd eat it."

"Yeah. If I were really hungry," Maggie nodded, her nose wrinkled in thought.

"Dane had a decent life. Or at least, he did. That is, until Otto Deitz blew the lid off," Gary said as they drove.

Maggie looked out the window, watching the beautiful scenery of Fair Haven's downtown. They passed The Bookish Café, which looked like it was doing just fine in her absence. No smoke, no flames, no people running for their lives out the front door. That was a good sign, she smirked.

"I don't see any fire trucks around the bookstore. They must be doing all right without you," Gary said. Maggie smiled wide.

"That's exactly what I was thinking," she chuckled.

As it turned out, Dane McKenny lived in a blooming subdivision just on the outskirts of town. Most trees were still kind of small. There were three architectural patterns of houses throughout, and the colors were all neutrals, making Maggie feel like she might be entering Stepford. The McKenny household was at the furthest end, at the tip of a cul-de-sac.

When Maggie saw all the kids' toys in the yard, her heart broke a little. What she'd read about in *Small Town Secrets* was not something children should know about their parents. Judging by the bikes and balls, the children at this house were still relatively small. Perhaps it could all blow over before they were old enough to understand.

The two-car garage door was open. There was a huge truck in the driveway. A green hose hung against the wall inside, along with an array of shovels, rakes, and brooms. A lawnmower was parked in one corner. A snowblower was in the opposite corner. Everything gleamed like it was brand new.

"All right. I'm going to go and talk to Dane.

Maybe his wife, too. But I only see one car, so I don't know who will answer the door. This could get ugly if she doesn't know what's happening. One of the most dangerous scenes a cop can walk into is a domestic dispute. I want you to stay in the car. No matter what you hear, stay in the car. Got it?"

Maggie raised her eyebrows. She hadn't expected Gary to be so serious. The tension squeezed her heart a little to know that he was going into what could very well be a volatile situation.

"Wait," she muttered. "I thought I got to come in with you."

"I said you could come along."

"You said I had to be quiet, but I could come with you."

"Yeah. I didn't realize what I'd said. Let's be honest. You can't be quiet. So just wait here. This won't take too long."

"Please be careful," she replied.

"I will," he winked. "Sit tight. I'll be back."

Maggie shook her head at his terrible Terminator impersonation. She watched as he walked up to the house, peeked in the garage, then made his way to the front door. Within seconds, as if he'd been waiting, Dane McKenny stepped out of the house. It was the same man who had knocked all of Otto's books off the table at the book signing. Maggie had no doubt. He looked just as angry, rubbing the back of his neck and shifting uneasily. He looked at the houses around him, perhaps to see if anyone was watching or peeking from behind their curtains. Maggie did the same and couldn't for sure say she saw anyone. But this was Fair Haven. It only took one set of eyes to spread the word that there was a squad car outside the McKenny residence and a police officer at their front door. Finally, as if there was no escaping the humiliation, Dane nodded, and he and Gary stepped inside.

Maggie scooted in her seat and spied on the neighbors, looking for anyone spying on her. It was at that moment she saw something unusual.

Two doors down were a family of garden gnomes arranged from biggest to smallest. There was a total of five of them, all wearing sunglasses and Hawaiian shirts. They were the tackiest things Maggie had ever seen. That's why when she read about them in *Small Town Secrets*, she was sure it was part of the author's creativity. No one in their right mind would have that many garden gnomes and display those ugly little statues so prominently. Yet there they were, lined up and staring at her from behind their black sunglasses. Was there a Green Bay Packers decoration in that yard, too? That's what the book had described. Maggie scanned the landscape and saw the tacky green and yellow colors for the Packers emblazoned on a piece of cheese. Cheddar heads. That's what Green Bay fans were called because Wisconsin was the dairy state. There were whirly-gigs and windsocks and half a dozen other cheap decorations in this yard that Otto Deitz had not bothered to disguise. Maggie studied the house and came to the conclusion that probably everyone else in town did, too. That was the home of Lora Foretree, aka Lisa Forhee. The woman Zane McGinny aka Dane McKenny was supposedly having an affair with. Since Dane was his own boss there was no "boss's wife" he was cheating with like in the book. It was a neighbor. Just as close and incestuous.

"Eww. A neighbor? How tacky," Maggie murmured. She studied the house and focused on the windows. There wasn't the slightest bit of movement. She was sure no one was inside. Still, it might be worth peeking around the house to see what else was there.

Not that Maggie expected to find a murder weapon. A rope or cord of some kind that had been used to strangle Otto. A bloodied candlestick or broom handle that had been used to beat him with. But it was only a matter of time before Gary would be talking to the woman who lived there anyway. Did he know she lived in the same cul-de-sac?

Before she could talk herself out of it, Maggie climbed out the passenger side of the squad car. Rather than make it look like she was up to no good, she decided to march purposefully to the gnome-infested yard. Without hesitating she walked to the front door and knocked.

What are you going to say? You can't question her like a police officer. If she killed Otto, she'll have no problem killing you, too. This was a boneheaded move, her conscience scolded. For a brief second Maggie thought she heard footsteps pounding to the front door but realized that it was the pounding of her heart in her chest.

After seconds turned into minutes and no one had come to the door, Maggie pressed her face up to the glass, cupping her hands around her eyes to see inside. There was no movement of any kind. Letting out a sigh of relief, Maggie felt emboldened to peek around some more.

A neighbor is going to see you and call the police to report a prowler. That inner voice was getting more annoying by the second.

But the closest cop to the scene is your bestie from high school. So it shouldn't be a problem. Except that you promised to stay in the car.

Maggie shook her head to dislodge that small voice and headed around the side of the house. She squared her shoulders and held up her chin as if she had every right to be where she was, doing what she was doing. Making her way to the backyard, Maggie found there was a large back deck with a chaise lounge, a couple of high-backed rattan chairs and at least two dozen more gnomes placed all over. Maggie shivered. She was sure each one of them was staring at her judgmentally and that tonight they'd make their way to her cottage to try and kill her.

"Get a hold of yourself," she hissed. Without waiting for one of those ceramic devils to start moving, she walked up the two steps to the deck and looked inside the sliding doors. Still, there was no movement of any kind. Bravely, with nerve she didn't know she had, Maggie knocked. Loudly.

Nothing. No movement. No sounds. She tried the door and nearly let out a yelp when it easily slid open. Looking over her shoulder, Maggie could see that one neighbor had a clear view of the back of Lora Foretree's house. The rest were obscured by trees.

You've come this far. Why stop now? she thought.

Stepping one foot inside the house, she called out, "Hello? Anyone home?"

She held her breath. If she was confronted, she'd tell Lora that she was interested in buying a house on the next block. Someone suggested she talk to the neighbors about the area. Perfect. That would be as good an excuse as saying she was snooping around because she knew Lora and Dane were having an affair because she read it in a book. After a couple of seconds, she let out her breath and stepped inside.

No one is going to believe you're house hunting. They'll think you're robbing the place. That's what they're going to believe, her gut warned. It was too late now. She was inside Lora Foretree's home.

The family room had a television, a sectional sofa, a leather recliner. Hanging on the wall was a framed poster of a Harley-Davidson motorcycle. To the right, Maggie made her way to the kitchen. It was open, with an island in the middle. All white. Dishes in the sink. A metal placard that read *Harley-Davidson Parking Only* hung over the counter.

"This woman will kill me if she finds me in here," Maggie muttered. A woman who rides a motorcycle is someone who isn't afraid of anything. Scanning the kitchen, she saw a card standing up on the table. The swirly script and big red hearts gave away what kind of card it was. Maggie picked it up and read the inside:

PEPPERMINT,

Remember when I gave you that nickname? I do. Like it was yesterday. No one does to me what you do. If only we'd met at a different time. We did what we had to do. I have no regrets. They can't cage our love for each other. I'm thinking of you always. Don't ever doubt that.

—Your true love

MAGGIE SHIVERED. This was dated just this morning. Dane must have dropped it off because the mail wouldn't deliver that fast.

To Maggie, adultery was one of those offenses that couldn't be overlooked. Maybe it was a weak moment. Maybe a fight at home. Maybe alcohol. But it didn't change the fact: it was just plain gross. This was even worse. Judging from the words written down, Dane and Lora had done something together that might put them both in a cage.

"Murder. Murder will put you in a cage. And I wouldn't want anyone to know my nickname was Peppermint," Maggie whispered. Carefully, she put the card back.

Looking at the clock, she gave herself five minutes to sweep the house and get back to the squad car. There was no reason to peruse the living or dining room unless she wanted to see what kind of biker memorabilia went with fine china. There were several photos on the wall of Lora wearing a leather biker jacket and boots, standing next to a shiny chrome monster on two wheels. She was not what Maggie expected.

Unlike the svelte seductresses Hollywood likes to portray mistresses as, Lora Foretree was a box-shaped woman with a red layered bob, a square jaw, and a worn-around-the-edges look. She had to be the wild side Dane had been yearning for in the middle of some kind of mid-life crisis. Maggie knew what Dane looked like. The business owner who dealt in meats and wore a suit to work wanted to experience something unlike what he was used to. That had to be it.

"Maybe Lora has a heart of gold," Maggie said

to herself as she went down the hallway to the bedrooms. The master bedroom was the first door on the right. It was a plain white room with a basic bedroom set that could be bought at any furniture store. Maggie wasn't sure why, but she'd half expected there to be leopard print bed covers and mirrors on the ceiling. It was just a normal bedroom.

The bathroom was attached. That was where Maggie first saw the blood.

It was like catching a glimpse of a fox while driving along the road. You see it, look away for a second, and wonder if you imagined it. But when Maggie blinked, the blood was still there on the floor. It wasn't a lot. But it was too much to ignore.

She couldn't say that she really wanted to see what was behind the shower curtain. However, Maggie was not about to leave without knowing. She'd already trespassed.

Yes. You're already where you shouldn't be. Now you're in a room where there's blood on the floor. And it leads to a shower. Might as well look, her thoughts stammered.

Maggie's mouth had gone bone dry. When she swallowed, it scratched like she was coming down with a cold. Her breath was shallow. As she reached for the shower curtain, she saw her hands trembling like they belonged to someone else. Someone older. Someone frail. That wasn't her hand. She wasn't really about to pull back the curtain, was she?

Gently, she pulled back the plastic curtain and saw Lora Foretree, fully clothed in the tub. She was dead.

Ironically, she was almost in the same position Otto Deitz had been when she looked at him on the floor of the elevator. There were bruises all over her and red marks along her neck.

Maggie let her breath out. It was bad enough someone else had been killed. The real problem now was figuring out how to tell Gary. She was supposed to have stayed in the car.

Chapter 9

Maggie watched as Gary's eyes narrowed while she told him what she found. She'd managed to sneak back to the car just seconds before he emerged from Dane's house. It felt like she'd been in Lora's house for hours.

"It was the house described in the book. Down to the gnomes," Maggie whispered, even though they were alone in the squad car. "If you'd read the book, you'd have seen it too. I'm telling you that whoever killed Otto also killed Lora. There is one common denominator in all of this, and you were just in his house." Maggie pointed to Dane's house.

"That might be true, but do you want to tell me

how I'm going to explain that I found Lora dead in her bathtub when I had no warrant, no reason to go inside the house? Can you come up with a reason that might be believable?" His jaw was tight.

After swallowing hard, Maggie shrugged. "Didn't he tell you that he was seeing Lora? They are having an affair, you know."

"He mentioned he had an affair and that it was over," Gary rubbed his eyes.

"What? He's lying. There is a love note in there dated today. He was over there, Gary."

"So he left a note but also decided to kill Lora on the same day?"

"Maybe they had a fight. I don't know. Does Dane have an alibi? Where is his wife?" Maggie's eyes nearly popped out of her head as she considered Dane's wife's position in all of this.

"Let me think a minute. Okay, here's what is going to happen. Did you touch anything in that house? Did you look in the fridge? Did you pick up any picture frames or rummage through any drawers?"

Maggie recoiled as if his words had suddenly grown legs and begun to wiggle.

"Rummage through her drawers? No. Why

would I do that? Look in her fridge? I should have. I wonder what she ate?"

Gary looked blankly at Maggie. "You are a mystery woman. I'm telling you that as a friend. Okay, I'm taking you to your car, and I want you to go directly home."

"What? Home? Why?"

"Oh, could it be because you can't be trusted to do something simple like sit in the car? Because I took a chance on taking you along to question a person of interest, and you managed to find a dead body. Do you think that could be it?"

"Fine. But I'll want to know exactly what happens when you are done. Come by my place and give me a debriefing," Maggie replied as she snapped her seatbelt across her lap and let out a deep breath.

"Debriefing. You really are something." Gary shook his head.

They rode most of the way in silence. Once at her car, Maggie hopped out and reminded her friend to come directly to her house once he was finished.

"It might take a couple of hours. But I will," Gary replied.

"Hey, if you solve this, will you get a promotion?" Maggie asked.

"Well, if I don't get fired for bringing a pleb along on a murder investigation, there might be something in it for me," he smirked.

Maggie pinched her lips together, turned on her heel. On the drive home, she was sure that there were more clues in the book. She was going to go through it with a fine-toothed comb. *Small Town Secrets*, indeed. The funny thing was, what Otto wrote about weren't really secrets at all. People had to know Dane and Lora were having an affair. There was also the character who drank on the sly while working at City Hall. And how could she forget the side story about the divorcée who said her husband left her, but no one could say for sure they saw him leave. Maggie's mind drummed up images of fresh concrete being poured into a mysterious patch of ground in someone's backyard.

"Get a hold of yourself, Mags. Not everyone in Fair Haven is a murderer," she soothed as she pulled onto her gravel driveway.

Once inside her house, she was happy to peel out of her clothes and stand under a warm shower for a few minutes. But the image of Lora Foretree lying in her bathtub quickly filled her mind. As if jolted by an electric shock, Maggie jumped out of the shower, shut off the water, and wrapped herself tightly in a robe. Then suddenly her memory was jarred.

"Oh, Mrs. Peacock," she huffed. She'd forgotten to park her car in the long driveway near the main house. If her car was in front of the cottage when workers showed up, Mrs. Peacock would be whining and squawking for days.

She weighed staying inside and just getting up early tomorrow to move her vehicle. But what if she overslept? That would be bad.

"Ugh!" she griped as she pulled on a pair of sweatpants and a T-shirt. No need for shoes. It was only going to take a second.

With her shoulders hunched like she was going on a five-mile trek in the snow, Maggie grabbed her keys and stepped outside. Her gravel driveway was more weeds and flattened stones. She tiptoed along, careful not to step on anything too jagged. The idea of running inside to slip into a pair of flip-flops or slippers crossed her mind, but she didn't want to waste any more time. Better to endure a few minutes of discomfort and get the job done than waste more time searching her cottage for flip-flops. It was already late and dark outside.

There were more pebbles and stones wanting to stick to the bottom of her feet on the driver's side of her car than there were in the driveway. Not to mention how dirty her feet were now going to be.

"That's your problem, Mags. You have the tendency not to think things through," she scolded as she turned the key in the ignition, backed out of her driveway, and then swung around to the main driveway leading up to the big house.

A motion light snapped on. Maggie thought she saw something move out of the corner of her eye. When she turned her head, there was nothing. It was probably a trick of the light.

Without thinking anything more of it, Maggie shut off her car. For a few seconds, she sat there and looked into Mrs. Peacock's house. There was a wall of windows across the back of her home. She was either in another part of her house or out at some dinner event being all glamorous, flashing her beautiful jewelry while complaining how she was on a fixed income.

Maggie wished she could be on Mrs. Peacock's fixed income. She'd been inside Mrs. Peacock's home more than once. It was as beautifully gaudy as Mrs. Peacock was. There were antiquities mixed with dollar store finds all over. Lovely works of art from local artists hung on the walls. Of course, there was a painting of Mrs. Peacock and her late husband hanging in the main entrance so everyone could see the face of the man who was responsible for her fixed income.

Maggie always thought they looked like an ideal couple. She was spontaneity to his stoicism. Perfect complements to one another.

Mrs. Peacock also had tons of books. That was one thing Maggie knew from the start. The old broad liked to read, even if she kept it a secret from most people. She was as book smart as she was street smart. A deadly combination for a woman.

After admiring the interior of the house, Maggie finally took her keys and climbed out of the car. The tiny pebbles she'd picked up in the car dug into the balls of her feet as she resorted to tiptoes again to walk along the driveway to the path through Mrs. Peacock's yard. It wasn't the worst pain she'd ever felt, but it was enough to make her lean on the car and wipe her feet off, if for no other reason than to get the current set of stones off, only to be replaced by a fresh set as she snuck back to her cottage.

That was when she heard it.

Breathing.

Maggie held her breath as she pretended to study her foot for a second. Yes. Someone was breathing. She could hear it. Every hair on her body rose up. Her senses were electrified, ready to soak up the slightest sound, smell, or movement.

Even though her mouth had gone dry, she licked her lips and tried not to look like she'd heard anything. The motion light did give her enough illumination to see a good portion of the driveway. But on the periphery, it was nearly black. There were jagged shadows along the garage and off into the tree line.

If you actually heard breathing, they aren't in the trees. They're closer, her mind whispered.

Maggie cleared her throat. She didn't know what to do. Should she run? Should she get back in her car? She held her breath and listened again. Maybe it was all in her imagination.

She stood there on one foot, wiping the stones away, not breathing as she listened. Nope. It was real. Whoever it was, wherever they were, they were breathing. In fact, a more horrifying thought popped into her head: they knew she was listening and had started to breathe even harder.

At that second, the motion light blinked out. Maggie heard shuffling feet and she darted in the direction of the backyard. The light popped back on just as a lumbering figure dressed all in black emerged from the shadow cast over the side door of the house.

Maggie yelped before breaking into a run. Her entire body became drenched in sweat, and her feet screamed in pain as she ran on the sidewalk. Stones, pebbles, and dirt retaliated against the tender flesh that slapped along the pavement. It wasn't because she wanted to, but because her body wouldn't let her continue. The pain had gotten so bad.

She slowed to a quick limp. Whoever was behind her had to be closing in. They were in shoes, after all.

Her cottage door was open. She was going to be found just like Lora Foretree. Strangled. Maybe beaten, too.

Her heart was pounding and a million things flashed in front of her. Why didn't she slip back inside and put on slippers? Why didn't she remember to park her car in the right spot? Why did she leave her house in the first place?

Just as she was sure the shadowy figure was closing in, a pair of headlights pulled into her drive-way. With a sudden burst of adrenaline, Maggie began to wave and shout.

Whoever had been a few steps behind her stopped, turned, and ran in the other direction. Maggie didn't feel the pain in her feet anymore. Someone was here to save her.

As she squinted, she saw it was Gary in the squad car. Why had he come so soon? He couldn't have finished inspecting Lora's house already.

Who cares? You're safe now. Safe! she thought.

All of these thoughts were nothing more than rational thinking seeping back in to calm her from the terror she'd just experienced. She was shaking and crying, and only when she collided with Gary, wrapping her arms tightly around him and letting the feeling of safety wash over her, was she able to speak.

"Mags? What in the world happened? Are you all right?" The worry in his voice was genuine as he stepped back, his hands still on her shoulders, looking her over for any injuries.

"Someone was chasing me. Someone was hiding in the shadows of Mrs. Peacock's place, and when I moved my car they came after me. Oh, ouch!" she grumbled as she tried to find a comfortable way to stand with the stones digging into her feet.

"What? Wait, start from the beginning," Gary

said as he took out his flashlight and shined it across the grounds.

At the very same time, they both saw a hooded figure duck down into the tall flowers Mrs. Peacock had growing in her yard.

"There! He's there!" Maggie pointed.

"Get in your house. Lock the door," Gary ordered, and began to slowly inch his way along the path, sweeping his flashlight back and forth, searching for the prowler.

Maggie did as she was told and limped pitifully to her cottage. Once inside, she turned on her porch light, locked the front door, and finally sat down on her favorite reading chair by the window.

She swept the pebbles from the soles of her feet and realized that she was bleeding from a gouge on her left foot. Something had caught her good, and she needed to clean the wound right away, but she was not going to leave her spot keeping an eye on Gary.

She saw his flashlight. As long as that was visible, he was okay.

What if there were more of them? What if there was someone else with this prowler who was waiting to jump out and pounce on Gary?

If there was more than one, they would have gotten you,

Mags. Nope. This is a lone wolf, she tried to comfort herself. But between the pain in her feet and the worry for Gary, she was beside herself.

That was when his flashlight went out.

Maggie froze. The only thing she could do was slowly reach up and tug the chain to extinguish the light inside the front room.

She listened and watched.

There was no noise. Just crickets chirping. The occasional scurry of something in the dried leaves and brush around the trees of her house.

No one was screaming. No one was crying. It was like everything had stopped. As if time was frozen and only Maggie was aware of it.

Then she heard footsteps.

Her heart pounded and again she began to sweat. First, she saw feet. Then legs. And finally, emerging from the darkness into the porch light, was Gary.

Pain and blood or not, she jumped up and dashed to the front door to open it for him.

He had a bit of sweat on his forehead, but other than that, he didn't seem shaken or concerned. Without a word, he pointed to the seat for Maggie to sit back down. Then he shook his head.

"Whoever that was, they're gone. Oh, Maggie,"

he gasped when he looked down and saw the bloody footprints on the floor.

"Oh. What a mess," she mumbled as tears stung her eyes. She told him she'd just taken a shower, and now she was all dirty all over again.

She was crying with fear, relief, anger, and frustration. All of it rolled out from inside her.

Chapter 10

"Who would be bothering me? I didn't have anything to do with Otto Deitz's gossip story. I'm not even in it. Why would anyone be following me? It's not like they know I'm snooping around," Maggie huffed as she sat in her living room, in her favorite reading chair by the window.

She couldn't be sure, but there might've been eyes peeking at her from the darkness. She searched and didn't see anything or anyone. It didn't matter. She stood and tugged at the cord for the blinds, which quickly descended with a final thud on the windowsill.

Gary had gone into the kitchen. Water was running in the sink. When he came back out,

Maggie had expected him to be holding cups of tea. Instead, he walked up to her and extended his hand. She took it, stood up, and winced. Before she could say anything, he scooped her up in his strong arms and carried her to the kitchen, where he set her on the counter by the sink.

"Put your feet in there," he said, pointing to the water that had partially filled the basin.

Maggie pulled up her pant legs and did as she was told. For a brief second, the water stung, but within seconds her feet felt better. Using her hand, she rubbed away the dirt and blood and realized that there wasn't really all that much damage. Just one major cut on the pad of her left foot, but even that was barely bleeding now.

Gary had disappeared down the hallway toward the bathroom. "Do you have band-aids?" he shouted.

"In the medicine cabinet," Maggie replied. After a couple of familiar sounds—mirror opening, things being shuffled—Maggie heard Gary gasp.

"What is it?"

"You use black toothpaste?" he called back, making Maggie's muscles relax. She started chuckling to herself.

"It's charcoal. It's supposed to be good for your

teeth," she replied, just before the medicine cabinet door shut and Gary reappeared with a box of band-aids and a hand towel over his shoulder.

"Yeah, well, they say rhubarb makes good pies too, but you'll never convince me of that," he joked as he stepped up to the sink and passed her the hand towel.

Maggie pulled her left foot out of the water and patted it dry while Gary inspected the wound. "That doesn't look so bad. No bigger than the hole in your head, and you function just fine with that."

"Very funny," she whined, smiling despite herself.

"Hey, do you remember that time in high school when we snuck out at one in the morning to watch that meteor shower?" Gary asked.

"Of course I remember that. That was fun. We saw tons of meteors. I don't think I know anyone who has seen more in their lifetime," Maggie said. "No one ever knew we did that, either."

"Nope. That's our secret," he said as he pulled the tabs off one band-aid and stuck it to her bare foot.

"Gary?"

"Yeah," he said, getting another band-aid ready as she dried her other foot.

"Do you think we'll always be friends like this? Like, even if we get married to other people and have kids and stuff?"

Gary grinned. "I think we will. But you're a strange bird, so I'll tell you what. When you're an old maid and I'm looking for my next trophy wife, we can tie the knot out of convenience. What do you say?"

"Very funny," Maggie chuckled. "I'm not going to be an old maid."

"That's what you think," Gary needled, before getting a smack on the arm.

"So, what happened at Lora's place? I'm assuming that's what took you so long to get here," Maggie said.

"I think we both know I got here just in time." Gary winked. "So, we better get comfortable because there's a lot of ground to cover. Do you have any food?"

Food? At the mere mention, Maggie's stomach growled. She hadn't eaten anything for hours. Carefully, she climbed down from the counter and pulled open her fridge.

Within a few minutes, Gary and Maggie were sitting at the kitchen table with peanut butter and jelly sandwiches, ridged potato chips, and chocolate milk at their fingertips.

"So how did you manage to get the ball rolling at Lora's house?" Maggie asked.

"Someone left the back door open," he said.

Maggie sighed and nodded. Okay. She did that.

"It was unlocked when I got there," she said, popping a chip in her mouth.

"Yeah, well, considering most people eat supper or watch television around the time you were breaking and entering, I think—"

"I didn't break anything!"

Gary chuckled again. "I think it's safe to assume you didn't kill Lora Foretree. The problem is going to be for Dane. His wife found out about his shenanigans."

"Obviously," Maggie replied with a mouthful.

"She took the kids and left for her mother's house in Calumet. He's been alone for the past three nights. Now, on the first day of the book fair, when you saw him having a temper tantrum, he'd been at work."

"That explains the suit," Maggie added.

"Yeah. But he said that even though Otto Deitz's book ruined his life, he didn't kill him. He admitted to wanting to beat his smug face in. But he wasn't a killer. So he said." Gary took a sip of chocolate milk.

"What do you think?" Maggie asked. "If security hadn't arrived at Otto Deitz's table when they did, I think the whole story might have begun and ended right then and there. He was going to tear him apart."

"That's what I said to Dane. Eyewitnesses said he was out of his mind. So, I pressed him on where he was at that time, and he said he was with Lora, breaking things off."

"You don't really believe him, do you?"

"I'm gonna have to," Gary said. "I can't confirm anything since she's dead."

"I think he killed them all," Maggie said. "He had motive to kill Otto. Maybe Lora didn't want to break up. You know these other women always think the guy they're cheating with will leave their wives to be with them. We don't know what Dane promised her. But I'll bet it didn't include strangling her and leaving her in the bathtub. After dropping off a love letter."

Gary chuckled. "For someone who not twenty minutes ago was shaken up pretty badly by a prowler, you haven't lost your sarcasm. And FYI: we don't know yet if she died of strangulation."

"She had marks on her neck. The same kind as Otto had."

"Yeah, but we can't rule anything out. Otto was cracked on the head, then strangled."

"Wait. You think it might be more than one person involved?"

"I don't know."

Just then, someone rang Maggie's doorbell. She jumped in her seat.

"Who would be here at this hour?" she whispered to Gary, who shrugged before pulling his gun from his holster.

Maggie went to the door. All the lights were on in the house. It wasn't like she could pretend they weren't there. She peeked out the peephole.

"Who is it?" Maggie barked like a pit bull.

"Agnes Krueger." The private detective barked back.

Gary let out a breath and holstered his gun.

Maggie opened the door and tilted her head at Agnes, squinting and grimacing as if she suddenly smelled something bad.

"Sorry to bother you so late. What's the matter? Do I smell?" Agnes asked, taking a step into the cottage.

"I don't know if you smell," Maggie replied flatly.

"Look, I know it's late, but I've got something to say. I'll say it and then I'll leave." Agnes straightened her blazer and lifted her chin.

For a moment, Maggie thought she might apologize for how she'd acted earlier, when she caught her trailing the two men from the hotel. No such luck.

Chapter 11

"What's this all about?" Gary asked.

"You two have been pretty busy tonight," Agnes replied. "First you leave the book fair, then you stop at Dane McKenny's house and Officer Brooks goes in. But Little Miss Nosey decides to sneak into Lora Foretree's house. Next thing I know, the officer is giving her a lift back to her secret parking spot and then heads back to gnome heaven, only to have backup and the coroner show up. It's all very curious."

"So?" Maggie crossed her arms over her chest. Gary put his hands in his pockets and waited for Agnes to continue.

"That's not a great look for the Fair Haven police, having a civilian snooping around a crime scene." Agnes looked around like she had misplaced her purse. "Mind if I sit?" she asked before dropping herself into Maggie's favorite reading chair, making Maggie wince.

"I think if it really bothered you, you would have made a call to my superiors. What's this really about?" Gary asked, his patience clearly wearing thin.

"Okay. I'm going to level with you. I've been in the private investigator business for about a year. I've done all right, mostly getting paid to spy on cheating spouses for divorce cases. This is the first time I've had a murder case on my hands."

Maggie thought there was a strange twinkle in her eye as she said this.

"That really doesn't have anything to do with us," Gary said.

"Technically, no. But did you know Heather McKenny hired me to snoop on her husband? I've got pictures of him with the now deceased Lora Foretree."

Maggie looked at Gary, who nodded and said, "We knew they were having an affair."

"Yeah. It's all in Otto Deitz's book," Maggie said. "And you said he hired you to keep an eye on things because he was getting threats. Who exactly are you working for?"

"I was working for Otto Deitz and Heather McKenny. Separately. They each got their own bill. Thankfully, Heather can continue to pay hers." Agnes leaned back in Maggie's chair like it was her own living room.

"Isn't that a conflict of interest?" Maggie asked without a second thought.

"Not anymore." She focused on Maggie. "You really do like to stick your nose where it doesn't belong. One of the things I keep noticing is that you're always around whenever something suspicious happens. Why do you think that is?"

Maggie squinted and twisted her mouth in mock contemplation. "Just lucky, I guess."

Agnes didn't appreciate the sarcasm. "I'm learning that these small towns are where the real action is. At that lake off Main Street, you could find a big rock on the shore and walk right past it without a second glance. But if you stop and turn it over, you might see things that make your skin crawl. Small towns are the villains hiding in plain sight."

"What do you want, Miss Krueger?" Gary asked.

"If I wrap up this murder case, it'll be the feather in my cap that makes me look like a peacock. I'm running out of jewelry to hock just to keep the lights on and gas in my car. This could mean a spectacular bump in my rates. How about we share some information?" She smirked.

Maggie swallowed and studied the private detective. Something about her felt off, but she couldn't put her finger on it. Well, other than the fact she was bossy and rude and threw her weight around like the town bully.

"What kind of information?" Gary asked, making Maggie whip her head in his direction.

He wasn't seriously going to cooperate with this woman, was he? She was awful. Why would he even entertain the idea? She'd practically admitted to spying on them and had the nerve to make their friendship sound like something shady.

Agnes smirked and licked her lips before leaning forward, resting her elbows on her knees. "Heather McKenny."

"We've spoken to Heather," Gary said. "She was at her mother's house after she found out about Dane's indiscretion and wasn't around when Otto was murdered. We checked her alibi. Her mother verified it."

"Yes, that checks out. But did you know Heather has a twin sister?" Agnes pulled out her phone and showed a photo. "Identical, not fraternal. Paige Marie Colpot. Lives one block from their mother. History of violence in past relationships. More than one restraining order has been filed and granted. She's a live wire nobody seems too interested in. Except me. And now, you."

Gary looked intrigued. He pulled out his notebook and started writing. Maggie looked back at Agnes, who winked at her. Maggie raised her right eyebrow but said nothing.

"Before I hand over anything, I'm going to have to verify it," Gary said. "You understand, right?"

"Of course. I'll be in touch. Your number is 9-1-1, right?"

"Something like that," Gary replied.

Just then Maggie snapped her fingers. "Hey, did you happen to see anyone lurking around the grounds earlier? There was someone on the property. Was that you?"

Agnes slowly shook her head, her expression turning serious. "No. I didn't see anyone. What happened?"

Maggie didn't want to tell her. She didn't trust Agnes, who seemed more interested in advancing her career than protecting anyone. But Gary apparently felt differently and jumped in to tell her.

"That's scary. See what happens when you try to plant a garden where the bodies are buried?" Agnes snickered.

"You do it for a living. What's the difference?" Maggie huffed.

Agnes stood and swept back her jacket, revealing the holstered stun gun she had flashed at the book fair parking lot. "It's a small difference. But this difference makes all the difference in the world." She clicked her tongue.

Maggie shuddered. The woman acted like she thought she was the star of her own crime show.

"All right. I'll verify the information," Gary cut in. "I've got your business card. I'll call once I've looked into it."

"You do that. Well, I've obviously overstayed my welcome, so I'll be on my way. Don't stay up too late, kids," she smirked, strutting out the door like she was in a Western. Maggie shut the door behind her and turned to Gary.

"Isn't there something really weird about that woman?"

"Yeah, she's odd all right. But this is something new. Paige Colpot. I've never heard the name before. Has anyone by that name ever come into the bookstore?"

Maggie frowned, pinching her brows together. "I could check. Mr. Whitfield kept a detailed mailing list. He did it the old-fashioned way until he finally dipped a toe into modern tech and made a database. But I don't think it's been updated since he..." Maggie shrugged.

"You still miss him a lot, don't you?" Gary asked gently.

She didn't speak. She just shrugged again, then nodded.

"Can you imagine what he'd say if he saw you going toe-to-toe with a private investigator, racing to solve a murder?"

"I'm not racing anyone," Maggie snapped.

"Who do you think you're talking to, Mags? The snippy comebacks, the look on your face. If you thought you could get away with it, you'd have clawed her eyes out. She's on your turf."

Maggie let out a long breath and rubbed her eyes. "I'm just tired. That's all. If she can wrap the case up fast, she should do it. If she can't, she needs to get out of our way."

"Our way?" Gary laughed as he stood in the

open doorway. The cool night air made Maggie cross her arms over her belly.

"Are you going home?" Maggie asked.

"Actually, I'm going to follow up on this lead. I'll check the grounds before I go. Just to be safe," he said, giving her a quick kiss on the top of her head. As he disappeared into the night, becoming no more than a moving beam of flashlight in the dark, Maggie shut the door behind him and locked it tight.

Chapter 12

The next morning, Maggie woke up to her alarm clock. Instead of taking her time to get ready for the last day of the book fair, she quickly threw herself together, grabbed her pass and purse, and sped over to The Bookish Café before it opened. It was a long shot that Paige Colpot was on their mailing list. Even if she was, what did that prove? That she read books?

"Well, someone in that family must read, because they saw what was in Otto Deitz's book and it blew up their world," Maggie muttered to herself at the steering wheel as she pulled up in front of the bookstore. "This is crazy. I'm up before the rooster, looking into this like there's actually going to be something helpful."

With the key around her neck, she opened the front door, setting off the jingling bell overhead. Poe looked up from his nap and squinted at her, as if to ask, *Why are you waking me at this ungodly hour?* She shut the door behind her and relocked it, then stepped over to Poe to scratch his head and nuzzle him after a couple of quick kisses.

"Good kitty," she said as he purred his approval of her affection.

Maggie left the lights off in the store as she carefully made her way to the cubby that had been Mr. Whitfield's office. It wasn't huge. Even though Joshua had done quite a bit of streamlining and updating the business, he seemed just as reluctant to move his father's things as Maggie had been. As if somehow, that would be finalizing the fact that he was never going to be there again. Of course, they knew that, but there was something comforting about seeing his sweater still hanging on the coat rack. His corny knickknacks and strange collectibles were handpicked by him. So, in a sense, he was still there with them, keeping an eye on things and hopefully enjoying the changes and developments in the business.

Swallowing hard, Maggie looked down to see

Poe had snaked his way around her legs, standing still with his body pressed against her calf.

"Poe, we need to see if Paige Colpot was on the mailing list here. I doubt it. But if she was, and that will give me an address to go check out. I don't know what it is, but I don't trust that Agnes Krueger." Maggie said, reaching down to give Poe one more quick scratch behind the ears before sitting in Mr. Whitfield's chair.

She pulled open the file cabinet and scanned the tabs.

"Mailing list. Oh my gosh, Poe. Would you look at this?" She chuckled as she pulled the bulky file out from the rest. "I can't believe all these people wanted Mr. Whitfield's little letter. I don't remember ever taking this many envelopes to the mailbox."

She tried to think of when he went digital and realized it had to have been not long after she started working there. Either way, she didn't have anything to do with it. It was his project. Maggie wasn't on the mailing list since she had the privilege of working there and getting a front-row seat to Mr. Whitfield's love of books and reading recommendations.

"Let's see. Please let these be in A-B-C order

and not some crazy numerical code method that they stopped using after World War II," Maggie muttered.

It was confusing. Some sections seemed to be in alphabetical order, but then it would switch to something else until Maggie finally realized the key.

"Month and name. Mr. Whitfield, sometimes your eccentricities went overboard."

With Poe now perched on a stack of paper on the bookshelf, Maggie managed to get a grip on the information and skipped to the most current couple of years. It was tedious, and she was afraid she might not get out of the bookstore before running into Babs, or maybe even Joshua. It wasn't that she was worried they'd be mad at her for rummaging around. She just didn't want to explain everything. It would take too long, and they'd ask all kinds of questions.

She still wanted to get to the book fair. The weekend pass didn't just fall from the sky. Maggie was determined to get her money's worth and enjoy all three days.

Just as her mind started to drift with the monotony of scanning each name for the one she was looking for, there it was.

"Oh my gosh! Paige Colpot! Poe, we found it,"

she whispered excitedly, waving the paper at the cat, who blinked, then yawned.

The address was listed as a house in Calumet, which was about half an hour away. The handwriting had lots of unnecessary loops and curls, like a teenager might have filled out the form. That's what made the line in the comments section all the more cryptic:

Favorite genre: true crime.

A shiver ran up Maggie's back. She looked over her shoulder, even though she knew no one was behind her. No one was anywhere near her. Just Poe.

Without waiting another minute, she folded the paper and stuffed it in her purse. After putting everything back where she'd found it, Maggie got up from the desk, petted Poe one last time, then left the store, locking it up tight behind her.

Now she had another dilemma: go to the book fair first, or drive to Calumet? While driving, Maggie carried on a conversation with herself that nearly came to blows. Until finally, the rational side took over.

"Otto and Lora are not going to be more or less dead depending on if you go to the book fair or not. You paid for the pass. No one's going to be mad or disappointed. Just go, and after the event, spin past Calumet and see what's shaking. There. Done and done."

Once again, her parking spot was waiting for her. As she pulled in, she saw the line at the front door of the convention center wasn't nearly as long as it had been on the first day. That made Maggie feel good, since it meant there would be more for her to pick over with fewer buyers to compete with.

But as soon as she got out of her car and took a step, she realized she wasn't alone.

"Hey! I know you!" came a familiar voice from behind her.

When Maggie turned around, she couldn't believe it. Her boss, who she'd tried to avoid just a short while earlier, was trotting up to her.

"Hi. Um... what are you doing here?" Her tone came out disappointed, even though she didn't mean for it to.

"I just thought I'd pay for a ticket and see what all the hubbub was about. Lots of people are coming into the store looking for the book written by that author who was just murdered. Did you hear about that?" Joshua asked innocently.

"Yeah. I was at the hotel when it happened. Wild," Maggie said, nodding, eyes wide.

"Wild indeed. I've had to put in an order for fifty more copies of that book. Have you read it? It's supposed to be pretty racy and all about Fair Haven. Talk about seeking revenge. Have you ever thought of writing a book to name names?" Joshua smiled as they walked toward the end of the line.

"Every day," Maggie replied with a straight face. Joshua laughed. Then she did too.

The ticket price for the last day was only twenty-five dollars, which Joshua thought was steep, but Maggie thought was reasonable. They walked in together, and Maggie told Joshua there were a couple booths she wanted to check right away.

"They've got some interesting titles I'm hoping no one picked up," Maggie said.

One stride of Joshua's equaled two of Maggie's as they hustled through the crowd. There was a display of vintage books offering four pulps for five dollars. Maggie couldn't pass it up. When she reached another display of coffee table books on sale, she scooped up the one on fly fishing lures, another on tools of the Civil War era, and a third on undergarments from the Middle Ages to today.

"Margaret Bell. I'm shocked you'd be interested in such a topic," Joshua teased. Maggie blushed and pinched her eyebrows together.

"Very funny. I guarantee this will be sold within two weeks for ten percent less than the price on the inside flap," Maggie said.

"You think so?"

"Yup," she said, handing her money to the vendor.

"Are you positive?"

"Three weeks tops," she replied, squinting up at him as she took the bag.

Joshua smirked. "Care to make it interesting?"

"What do you mean?"

"I'll bet you that it will *not* get sold in three weeks. It'll sit with the other unique titles for at least six months," Joshua said, making Maggie chuckle, roll her eyes, and shake her head no.

"Okay. What's the wager?"

"If you win, and the book is off the shelf in two weeks, I owe you lunch from Carmine's Ristorante."

"Deal. If I lose?"

"If you lose..." Joshua tapped his chin, squinted, and pouted his lips before finally looking down at Maggie and smirking. "You have me to your place for dinner. Home-cooked."

"What? You know I don't know how to cook. I mean, I know how to cook for *myself*. Tuna fish sandwiches and maybe tomato soup. Peanut butter and jelly on crackers."

"With all the cookbooks we have at the café, and you never picked one up to try a couple recipes? Why, Margaret Bell, I'm downright shocked," Joshua teased.

"It is rather shocking," Maggie mumbled.

"Well, I feel that makes this wager even more exciting. I'll tell you what. When I win—and I *will* win—you don't have to cook beef Wellington or anything. Spaghetti and meatballs will be good. I'll put in my request now."

"Fine. But you'll be getting it from Carmine's restaurant," Maggie huffed and made her way to the next booth, handing the bags to Joshua to carry. She didn't want him to see how nervous he'd just made her.

"Why are you in such a hurry?" he asked, carrying the heavy books as if they weighed no more than a sack of oranges.

"Oh, uh, I just don't want anyone to grab the stuff I want. And you probably want to get back to the café and make sure things are running smoothly. You know how things always go wrong when the boss is gone," she rambled.

"I think Casper can handle everything. Why? Are you trying to get rid of me?"

"No," Maggie blurted out—too quickly. Joshua smiled.

"How about when we're done here, we go grab something to eat?" he said casually.

Maggie's mind raced. She'd already made plans for the day. She had a temperamental twin with a violent history to spy on. However, Joshua had just asked her to lunch. Not a date-date, but still. Showing up where he knew she'd be, acting inter- ested in her hobby, and now suggesting a meal together? That was a pretty clear signal he was interested in... something.

Maggie swallowed hard. "I've kind of got plans after this," she said quickly, pushing her glasses up her nose and avoiding eye contact.

"Oh. Okay," he said. The disappointment in his voice was unmistakable. Maggie's heart pounded. What was she doing? She liked him. He was tall and strong, with broad shoulders and a scruffy jaw that was rugged and charming.

"I'd really like to, but I already made plans, and I can't break them. If I do, I might never get the chance again," she said, sounding more like a film noir heroine than someone turning down lunch.

When she finally looked up, Joshua was staring at her like she'd sprouted antlers.

"What are you up to, Maggie?"

"What? Me? Nothing. That's crazy talk," she stammered.

"Now I know you're lying. Maggie, are you in trouble? Because I can help. Whatever it is, I'd be happy to."

The look of concern on his face made her chest ache. The guilt was too much. She clicked her tongue, planted her hands on her hips, and looked down at her feet. Then, deep breath. No getting out of it; he wasn't going to let her off the hook.

"I'm going to... spy on someone," she admitted.

"Spy?"

"Yes."

"What for?"

She cleared her throat. "It has to do with Otto Deitz."

"Who?"

Maggie cupped her hand around her mouth, lowering her voice. "The author who was murdered. It's just a person of interest. I'm not saying she did it. I just want to see what she's up to. Maybe... snoop a little. Maybe."

Now it was Joshua's turn to put his hands on his

hips and shift his weight. "That sounds reckless and dangerous."

"And that's why I can't go to lunch."

"Oh, I think we can pick something up to go," he said, nodding. "You like McDonald's, right? Big Mac and fries?"

"What?"

"We'll get it to go. Eat in the car like real private investigators while we scope out the terrain. Okay, let's go." He hoisted the bag over his shoulder like a field pack.

"I don't think you're cut out for this kind of task," Maggie said, eyebrow arched. Truth was, she knew he could totally handle it, and she was thrilled. But no way was she going to let him know that.

"We're just going to have to see about that. Do you still want to walk the rest of the book fair? Because now that I know what you're up to, I'm not letting you go alone," Joshua said. "You're stuck with me."

Maggie's heart jumped. His breath in her ear made her shiver, and there was no stopping the smirk that crept across her lips.

"There's one more place I want to stop at, and then we can go. Are you buying McDonald's?"

"Yeah. I'll buy," he said with a smile. "I don't believe this."

"What? You offered," Maggie huffed.

"No, it's not that. I just thought I'd come to this book fair and chat with you for a while. I should've known you'd turn it into an adventure I never saw coming."

With a quiet flicker of pride, Maggie squinted and pushed her glasses up. They finished browsing the fair, Maggie buying a couple more titles for herself, and even offering to buy Joshua an old Philip Marlowe pulp.

"You can read it in the car while we're staking out my person of interest. Really get in the mood. You might even learn a thing or two," she said, deadpan.

"Ha!" Joshua laughed out loud.

The banter continued from the convention center to Maggie's car, to McDonald's, and all the way until they parked at the end of Kyle Street in Calumet, where Paige Colpot lived.

Chapter 13

After devouring her burger and fries, washing it down with a Coke, and flipping casually through her new books while periodically looking up at the small house, Maggie yawned.

"How long are we going to sit here?" Joshua asked.

"I don't know," she confessed. "I'm debating whether I should go look around. The last time I did at Lora Foretree's house, it didn't turn out all that well." She shivered at the thought of her lying dead in her tub as the image came sharply into focus.

"What happened?" Joshua asked, taking a sip of his Coke.

"She was dead in the tub," Maggie replied, as casually as if she were ordering another Big Mac.

"What?"

"Don't tell anybody."

"You're joking. Maggie. Tell me you're joking." Joshua stared at her.

"Well, I didn't do it," she said. "I found her like that. And I told the police immediately."

"Did you? Well, I suppose it's good to know you didn't just leave." Joshua rolled his eyes. "Maggie, you need someone to keep an eye on you. Do you realize how worried I'm going to be every time you leave the café? Wondering if you've gotten yourself mixed up with some mafia boss or accidentally stumbled into an arms exchange or counterfeit diamond deal?"

"Come on, Joshua. You know Fair Haven doesn't have that much going on." She crossed her arms and focused on Paige's house.

"You're not going to listen to me, are you?"

Maggie wrinkled her nose and squinted at the house. She wanted to look at Joshua, but knew if she did, she'd blush and stammer and nervously pick at a hangnail on her thumb.

"You don't need to worry about me," she said quietly.

"Hey, I do think any situation you get yourself into, you'll get yourself out of. That's the crazy thing about you. One of the things I lo—" Joshua cleared his throat.

Maggie stayed focused on the house, but inside, every nerve in her body vibrated like a sleepy engine after jumper cables had been attached. What did Joshua just almost say? She held her breath and didn't dare look at him. She waited. Was he going to say that one word? That heavy, weighted, four-letter word that could either heal or cripple a person?

No. He didn't mean that. He barely knew her. Aside from work, what did Joshua Whitfield really know about Margaret Bell? She liked books, made pretty window displays, and occasionally stumbled into trouble. Always someone else's trouble.

"I'm sure you can handle yourself," Joshua resumed. "If you can't physically beat someone, you'll definitely baffle them with sarcasm and ten-dollar words long enough to sprint. That's for sure."

It was the sweetest compliment she'd ever received. Her cheeks blazed. What should she do now? Look at him? Reach for his hand? Kiss him? Throw caution to the wind and do what she'd wanted to do since the day he showed up wearing his toolbelt at the bookstore, making all the changes she was sure she'd hate.

In her head, she was carrying on a conversation so intense she didn't realize she was moving her lips, making expressions, tilting her head from side to side while her eyebrows bounced.

"What are you doing?" Joshua asked.

"I'm talking things out with myself," she snapped, glancing at him before refocusing on Paige's house.

Just then, the front door opened. Maggie froze. Everything stilled except her hand as it lifted and pointed. Joshua was about to speak but stopped and followed her gaze.

The woman standing in the doorway, glaring right at them, was the same woman who had helped Maggie pick up Otto's books after her sister's husband knocked them to the floor. Did Dane McKenny not notice her? Were they both there and simply ignored each other?

Paige was definitely aware of Maggie and Joshua now.

She was muttering, talking to herself, just like Maggie had done seconds earlier.

"She sees us," Joshua said.

"What do we do?" Maggie asked.

"This is your rodeo. You mean you didn't have a plan?"

Maggie snapped her head toward him, then back to Paige. Swallowing hard, she opened her door and climbed out. Joshua followed.

"Hi," Maggie said awkwardly. "Um, are you Paige...?"

"You know who I am. Are you with that woman? I told her if she set foot on my property again, I'd cut her up and feed her to my dog."

Maggie stopped. Joshua froze as well. "What woman?"

Paige's eyes narrowed as she sized them up. "That private investigator."

Agnes Krueger had conveniently left out the part where she'd been confronted by the woman she was investigating. Maggie wasn't surprised. It would have bruised Agnes's ego, and that, Maggie suspected, was the one injury the P.I. couldn't tolerate.

"No. We're not with her. Or anyone. I saw you at the book fair. And at G's restaurant during the author meet and greet." At those words, the woman bristled. She clearly hadn't expected anyone to recognize her from both events.

"I didn't speak to you," she replied. "I don't

know who you are. You need to get off my property. I'm paying rent here, so I can say who's welcome and who isn't. And if you don't turn around right now, I'll call the police."

Paige was a peculiar character. Her spray tan practically glowed. Without teased hair and with a plain ponytail instead, she looked smaller, hardly the type Maggie would associate with restraining orders. But she might have that woman-scorned strength that surfaces after a drink or two.

"We better go," Joshua said, gently touching Maggie's arm.

"I know you had an issue with Otto Deitz for what he wrote about your brother-in-law," Maggie blurted out. "His mistress was just found dead. I thought you might want to know that."

"Wait. Who is dead?"

Maggie stopped and looked up at Joshua, then turned to face Paige.

"Well, Otto Deitz is dead. And Lora Foretree was just found dead."

Paige didn't look guilty. She looked annoyed, like this news was going to complicate her life, and not in a good way.

"Lora Foretree is dead?" she asked.

"Yes. Can I talk to you?" Maggie called out from the middle of the street.

"Who are you?" Paige demanded.

With a nervous cough, Maggie gave her name and repeated that she'd seen her twice before.

"So what are you here for? I didn't kill Lora."

"I didn't think you did," Maggie lied. "But Otto Deitz is dead too, and I saw you near him. Twice."

"That means you were near him. Twice," Paige snapped back. She had a point, and she knew it, arms crossed, chin lifted.

"You've got me there." Maggie had to admit Paige kind of scared her. She took a small step back without realizing it.

"You seem harmless. But let me tell you right now, if you're out here snooping for that witch with the stun gun, you're barking up the wrong tree."

Maggie started to respond, but Paige held up a hand.

"I knew my brother-in-law was having an affair long before Otto Deitz wrote about it. I confronted him at my nephew's fifth birthday party. That's what got the restraining order against me. My own sister signed off on it. Can you believe that?"

"Why would she do that?"

Paige shrugged. "She didn't want to believe it. At first."

"Why do you think Otto wrote about your brother-in-law's affair?" Maggie asked, hoping Paige would keep talking.

"It makes for good reading, don't you think? And Otto and my sister Heather had known each other for years before she married Dane. I think he was sweet on her. But once she picked Dane, Otto got bitter. It was time for him to let it go. They've been married almost eight years. When you're dead, lie down."

"Did you tell this to Agnes Krueger?"

"Who?"

"Agnes Krueger. The private investigator with the stun gun?" Maggie asked, lifting her eyebrows.

"No. She came storming in here like Dirty Harry with that thing, as if I wasn't used to trouble. I wasn't telling her anything. But you, well, you don't look like you'd hurt a fly. At least not the traditional way. I could be wrong, but usually I'm not. Just like I wasn't wrong about Dane or Lora. As for Otto Deitz," Paige shrugged. "My sister might know more. She's at our mom's place. Go bother her for a while."

Paige rattled off the address, then stepped back

inside and shut the door. Maggie heard the lock click. The conversation was over.

Maggie hurried back to the car, and Joshua followed.

"She said to go talk to her sister and mother," Maggie said, scribbling the address before she forgot it. "They live a little ways from here. Ready?"

"No."

"What do you mean no?"

"I've still got work to do, Mags. I can't play Sherlock Holmes with you all day. But I'll make you a deal. I'll rearrange my schedule tomorrow and go with you wherever you need to go. Besides, the longer you wait to shelve that book, the less chance you have of winning our bet. Don't forget."

He winked. He was right. Maggie started the car without a word and drove back to the bookstore.

"You promise you're not going to get into any trouble without me?" Joshua asked.

Maggie promised. But Serafina Lawson made no such promise. It didn't take long for Maggie to find herself in a very strange situation.

Chapter 14

Maggie pulled her car to the top of Mrs. Peacock's driveway and immediately noticed a red Lexus she didn't recognize. She'd never seen it before and wondered who it belonged to. Sticking to her usual routine, she walked quickly through the garden toward her cottage. It was still light out, but Maggie couldn't help but glance around nervously. She hadn't forgotten the attempted abduction the other night, and a bold daylight kidnapping or worse didn't seem entirely off the table.

When she reached her stoop, she stopped short. Her gravel driveway looked like it had been hit by a bomb. Dirt was torn up in patches, and along the street were the smallest CAT machines she'd ever seen: a mini digger, a tiny forklift. Funny, parking her car in the driveway had once been called an eyesore, but heavy machinery was apparently acceptable.

"Well, this is a sight," Maggie muttered aloud.

"What was that?" came a voice behind her.

Maggie jumped and spun around. Hand to chest, she let out a shaky breath. "Mrs. Peacock! I didn't see you. You scared me."

"I'm sorry, dear. I just wanted to let you know the men will be back tomorrow to finish up." Mrs. Peacock waved a hand toward the churned-up driveway. "They say it should be done by the weekend. Normally it only takes a couple of days, but since they're squeezing me in as a special favor, I'm at a slight disadvantage. Paying cash should speed things up."

"It's okay," Maggie nodded. "Do you have a visitor?"

"Oh yes. It's Serafina Lawson. She's in hiding. How you hide in a bright red car wearing matching red dress, I don't know, but that's what she claims she's doing. Why don't you get cleaned up and come out to the patio? We're having mint juleps."

Maggie's eyes widened, but she agreed. Once inside her cottage, though, she paused. What did

Mrs. Peacock mean, 'clean up'? She wasn't dirty. Her clothes were simple but neat. She checked her reflection: hair in place, no smeared makeup. With a shrug, she changed into a beige sundress that was casual and formless, something she usually wore on quiet weekends spent doing laundry or reading.

As she approached the patio, the scene was exactly what she expected. Mrs. Peacock in her flowing pink muumuu. Fifi in a red dress cinched tightly at the waist.

"Well, hello, honey," Fifi greeted her cheerfully. "When Vivian told me you'd extended a welcome, I just had to stop by before I left town. I was hoping to see you too."

"Hi," Maggie said awkwardly, giving a quick wave before sitting on an elaborate wicker ottoman with a green cushion.

"You're not leaving just yet," Mrs. Peacock said, turning to Fifi. "You're staying here for another day or two, and we're going to catch up. Mi casa, su casa."

"Oh, I couldn't impose."

"Nonsense. It's no imposition at all. Besides, it'll give that hormone-driven fan of yours time to cool down. I don't know how you put up with it," Mrs. Peacock said, sipping her drink. She didn't ask

Maggie if she wanted one, though Maggie didn't mind. Mint juleps were strong. With her limited alcohol tolerance, three sips might have her blurting out her thoughts on Mrs. Peacock's fixed income.

"Trent? He's harmless. It's this other situation that has me a little more curious," Fifi said, turning to Maggie. "You were there. What do you think about poor Mr. Deitz? That man had an enemies list as long as your arm."

"No one deserves to be killed the way he was. But you might be right. I read his book, and it literally named names," Maggie said, then cleared her throat.

"Have you read it, Fifi dear?" Mrs. Peacock asked.

"I haven't. Not enough spice for me. Besides, we all grew up in this town. I figured there wouldn't be anything in there I didn't already know or suspect. It was his fourth book, right? I'd be more interested in the early ones. Personal revenge never turns out the way you think," she said, winking at Maggie.

"Well, I'll tell you, it wasn't that great. And he didn't include anything about my husband, and that man practically built Fair Haven into what it is today." Mrs. Peacock pouted.

"Oh, darling," Fifi cooed. "Maybe that's your

sign to write a book about your beloved. Just make sure you include how you used to meet him behind the church after Sunday service."

"You do talk scandalous!" Mrs. Peacock whooped, bursting into laughter unlike anything Maggie had ever seen from her. Her eyes twinkled mischievously and her cheeks flushed red with glee. Maggie sat frozen, wide-eyed and slack-jawed, which only made the women laugh harder.

"Seriously," Fifi continued, catching her breath, "I don't know why anyone would be offended by being written about in a book. I'd be flattered. What do you think?" She turned to Maggie.

"I read the book," Maggie said carefully. "Otto didn't try very hard to disguise anyone. But I enjoyed it. I wouldn't call it Hemingway, but there's nothing like a redemption story to make you feel good."

"Oh, come on. It wasn't redemption, it was revenge," Mrs. Peacock said, waving her hand. "The character got what he wanted. The woman was destroyed. Her boy-toy fled town. The embezzler was caught. And the family that never understood him was left shouting after him like in that old Western... what was it? 'Come back, Shane!' Deitz wanted to prove something to everyone, and he did. He died for it."

"That's true," Maggie nodded, shifting on the small ottoman in hopes of finding a more comfortable position. It didn't help. Still, as she tried to perch on the too-small cushion, an idea sparked.

"Miss Lawson, if you're staying with Mrs. Peacock for a few more days, would you be interested in doing a book signing at The Bookish Café? I work there, and I'm sure Joshua Whitfield, the owner, would be happy to host you."

Fifi looked up, then over at Mrs. Peacock. "That sounds delightful. I'd love to. Since I'm staying with my dear friend, I don't see any problem at all. Count me in." She smiled and took another sip of her drink. Still, no one offered Maggie anything.

"Great. I'll get everything arranged. I've got Mrs. Peacock's number, so I'll call with the details."

"That sounds just lovely," Fifi said.

"Do I have to stand in line for a signed copy?" Mrs. Peacock teased. "You know how I abhor a crowd."

"Please, honey. If a dozen people show up, I'll be thrilled."

"You had a nice turnout at the book fair.

Everyone kept drifting toward your booth, even after all the drama," Maggie said encouragingly.

"Did you see that woman with the hair?" Fifi asked. "I saw her at three events leading up to Fair Haven. Serious Otto Deitz fan. I didn't know people like that existed for his kind of writing, but I've been wrong before."

Maggie had seen her. In fact, she'd just finished talking to her. Fifi might be comforted to know the woman's hair wasn't always that high.

"She was at the meet-and-greet, too. Just before Otto was found," Maggie added.

"He wasn't the only one who died," Maggie said quietly.

Both women turned to her. Fifi leaned forward, squinting.

"I suspected there was more to you than meets the eye," she said with a knowing smile.

Maggie sighed and shared that the police found Lora Foretree dead under mysterious circumstances. She left out names and specific locations and made them both promise to keep it to themselves.

"That includes Mrs. Donovan," Maggie added, pointing at Mrs. Peacock.

"Are you still talking to that mealy-mouthed

ninny?" Fifi asked, raising a brow high into her hairline. "After what she tried to do?"

"That was a long time ago, Fifi. And you never liked her."

"She won't like you either when she finds out I've been staying here," Fifi said. "You read Otto Deitz's book. Did he mention the saintly Donovan family at all?"

"No. He didn't," Maggie answered.

"Oh, now that's a book waiting to be written," Fifi scoffed. "That family alone could fill ten volumes. Deitz missed his chance."

"You stop spreading rumors, Serafina Lawson," Mrs. Peacock giggled.

"What rumors?" Fifi said. "It's all true. Well... maybe not who Reginald Donovan's real father is. People say it's old droopy-jowl Max, but I've got my doubts."

"Yes, most of us do. But far be it for me to entertain such gossip," Mrs. Peacock said, glancing out over her garden.

Maggie nearly choked on air. She had just told them she'd found another body possibly tied to a murder, and they were more interested in family scandal. Somehow, that made her feel safer. If they were this wrapped up in the Donovans, they were unlikely to breathe a word about the case.

"What did Mrs. Donovan do to you, Mrs. Peacock?" Maggie asked innocently. Unlike her landlord, Maggie wasn't one to tiptoe around a subject in hopes of gathering a few crumbs. She preferred to stick her face straight into the cake and take a bite.

"Oh, don't listen to Miss Lawson," Mrs. Peacock replied, waving her hand. "She has a tendency to make mountains out of molehills. That's why she's such a good writer." She took a long sip from her silver goblet, the sprig of mint sticking out like a garnish on a sundae.

"Vivian, don't fib to the girl."

"I'm not fibbing. I'm not saying anything," Mrs. Peacock said with a shrug, her eyes darting everywhere but at Maggie or Fifi.

Maggie wrinkled her nose. Maybe they were just messing with her. Maybe there was no secret, no scandal. Still, once she had Fifi at the bookstore and could get her alone, she might press a little harder and see what spilled out. For now, she was ready to get inside, lock her door, and decompress. She had her goodies from the book fair and intended to enjoy them.

With renewed energy, she excused herself from the ladies and confirmed one last time that she'd be in touch about the book signing. As she turned to leave, Fifi said something strange.

"Have a good night, honey. And make sure to lock your doors."

Maggie smiled and waved. But the words lingered. She hugged her bag of books closer and glanced over her shoulder. Both women were still waving. A few more steps, and the conversation behind her dropped to a whisper.

Were they talking about her? Maybe it was about Mrs. Donovan. Or the Donovan family in general. Or maybe it really was about Maggie.

"Stop being paranoid," she muttered. "Fifi couldn't chase you like that shadow man did the other night. Not in those heels."

She let herself into her cottage and quickly locked the door. But her breath caught. She remembered Fifi at the meet-and-greet. It wasn't Fifi that held her focus though. It was Trent, the clingy companion.

Her heart thudding, Maggie dropped into her favorite reading chair. She set her bags on the floor and tried to gather her thoughts. Trent had been tall. Thin. Like the figure she saw in the shadows.

He'd been with Fifi at the event and got angry when she dismissed him. Where had he gone after that?

She remembered him at the bar. He'd thrown back a drink. After that, she'd been deep in conversation with Otto and lost track of him. She only recalled seeing him again when Fifi discovered Otto's body. He came running, disheveled. But where had he been before that?

Fifi had been nearly hysterical. Maggie didn't believe she had anything to do with Otto's death. But maybe something in Otto's book struck a nerve. Trent was obsessed with Fifi. Rejected, drunk, and jealous. That was a dangerous mix.

"But what about Lora Foretree?" Maggie whispered. "How does she fit in?"

She headed into the kitchen and made herself a cup of tea. There was still some coffee cake left from when she and Gary had gone over the case. She'd need to talk to him again, see if he had any insight on Trent. Or Lora. Or both.

Excitement tingled under her skin. She took a bite of cake and called Gary mid-chew, launching into a recap of everything on her mind.

"And make sure no one's following you," she added.

"Who would be following me? I'm not the one

harassing Heather McKenny's twin sister," Gary teased.

"No one was harassing anybody. Do you want to hear what I have to say or not?"

"Fine, fine. I'll stop home, take a shower, and then come over. I'm off duty tomorrow anyway, though I have a feeling whatever you're about to tell me will keep me on the clock."

But by the time nine o'clock rolled around and he still hadn't shown or called, her nerves kicked in. She called and received no answer. She checked the station. No one had seen or heard from him since he'd clocked out.

Against her better judgment, she went looking for him.

She drove to his place. It was a small unit in a row of five apartments, just ten minutes from the bookstore. She'd only been there once, back when he first moved in, almost a decade ago.

Chapter 15

When Maggie pulled into the guest parking space near Gary's unit, she let out a small sigh of relief. His squad car was parked where it always was, and the lights in his apartment were on. But something felt off. There was no movement inside, no shifting shadows, no flicker from the television.

She considered honking the horn but looked around the quiet neighborhood and decided against it. Instead, she cut the engine, stepped out of the car, and walked up to the front door.

It was slightly ajar.

Maggie froze. The open door felt like an invitation, and not the good kind. Still, she knocked loudly, called out Gary's name, and waited.

"You better say something or I'm going to shoot the first thing that moves with my... Smith and Wesson... twenty-two Magnum," she called into the apartment, her voice shaking just enough to make it sound serious.

Holding her breath, she stepped inside.

That's when she heard a commotion from the bathroom.

"Gary?" she called again, louder this time.

No answer.

Keeping the front door open behind her, she crept down the short hallway toward the noise. The bathroom door was ajar, and just as she reached it, she caught a glimpse of a leg sliding out the small window.

"OH!" she screamed, just as the figure vanished over the sill and out of sight.

Panicked, she darted into the bedroom, then back to the bathroom, as if the intruder might've somehow doubled back. With no better option, she grabbed the plunger from beside the toilet.

If the trespasser came back, she was ready. Maybe he'd kill her, but not before getting a face full of toilet rubber.

Weapon raised, she crept back toward the front

room. Her heart was thudding. Every nerve was on edge.

That was the exact moment Gary walked through the front door, weapon drawn.

"Holy moly, Maggie! What are you doing here?" he yelled, lowering his gun as soon as he saw her. He leaned against the doorframe, exhaling hard.

"I came looking for you. You forgot we were supposed to meet earlier. I had tuna fish sandwiches all ready. Well... I had the cans out of the cupboard," she admitted. "When I got here, the door was open. I thought something happened to you."

"Maggie, come on. If you see a door open that's supposed to be closed, you don't go in. You call for backup," Gary said, his voice stern.

"But I thought you were in trouble," she said, her voice small. Now that he was home and safe, the full weight of the situation hit her, and her eyes filled with tears. "I'm sorry. I wasn't thinking."

Gary's expression softened. "Hey. I'm sorry I barked at you. It's been a long day. Yeah, I was supposed to meet you. But Agnes Krueger is in the hospital. Not dead, but she got her clock cleaned pretty good. I spent the evening talking to her. Then

I had to get back to the station, and every time I tried to call you, something else came up."

"If I'd called, you wouldn't have come here. Mags, I'm sorry."

He pulled her into a side hug, his arm resting naturally around her shoulders. It was warm and comforting, like a cup of tea.

"That really was stupid of me," she whispered, hugging him back.

"Well, in all fairness, you do have a history of walking into places you shouldn't. It's kind of your thing."

She looked up at him, saw the smirk on his face, and rolled her eyes. "Someone was here. When I got here, they were in the bathroom. I saw them climb out the window."

"Them?"

"Him. Or maybe her?" she said, hesitating.

Gary moved down the hall, gun in hand. Maggie followed slowly, careful to stay behind him.

"Is anyone still there?" she asked.

The moment the words left her mouth, she regretted them. What kind of question was that? Was Gary supposed to say, "Oh yeah, the burglar's still here. Just giving me a list of what he took."

"No. They're long gone by now," he replied, his voice low and steady.

"I didn't see if he took anything," Maggie said, glancing toward the living room. "Your television's still here. Do you have anything valuable? Jewelry? Watches?"

"Nah," Gary sighed. "Not really. But I *did* have one thing that mattered, and..."

He walked past her into the living room, then let out a frustrated groan. "This isn't good."

"What?"

Gary turned and planted his hands on his hips. "I had my notes. Some photos from the Otto Deitz case. They're gone."

Maggie's brow furrowed. "Do you think this is tied to Agnes Krueger? Why is she in the hospital anyway?"

"She was pretty out of it when I tried to get a statement. I'll have to go back tomorrow and sort things out. But it looks like she was nosing around Lora Foretree's place and ran into someone. I don't know who."

"But I bet we can guess," Maggie huffed. "Who else would be snooping around that house? The criminal returning to the scene of the crime. But why?"

"Slow down, Sherlock. That place had squad cars, an ambulance, and a coroner all over it a few hours ago. Anyone with half a brain could tell it was empty. Doesn't mean it was *our* guy. Still..." He gave her a look. "I'm inclined to agree with you."

"Agnes Krueger," Maggie whispered, placing a hand at her throat. "The poor thing."

"Her stun gun's gone, too."

"That's like Dirty Harry without his revolver," Maggie muttered, letting out a shaky breath. She didn't care much for Agnes' attitude, but the idea of her getting attacked stirred something protective in her. Maybe she'd bring her flowers. And gently ask a few pointed questions.

"How long will she be in the hospital?"

"At least overnight. Concussion."

"Oh no. He hit her?"

"Maybe. Or she fell. There was something about stairs. It's not clear yet." Gary scanned the room, taking in the scene. "This is the cherry on top of a long, lousy day."

"Looks like you need to file a report, too," Maggie said, scanning his apartment. "Do you think the same person who broke in is the one who attacked Agnes?"

"If it's not the same person, they're definitely connected."

"What do we do now?"

"We?" Gary raised an eyebrow.

"Yes, *we*," Maggie insisted.

A moment later, she found herself being ushered into the driver's seat of her car. She pouted, arms crossed, her eyebrows nearly touching.

"Mags, it's late. You've had enough of a scare tonight. I'm calling the station. Someone will come out here soon. I'll be asleep within the hour."

"You're going to sleep here? With a busted lock?"

"They got what they came for. No one's coming back."

"Gary, that's not safe. Come stay at my place. I'll wait with you for the officers and then you can crash on my... loveseat?"

Gary laughed. "I'm three feet longer than that thing. It's not even comfortable to sit on, let alone sleep on."

"Hey, it's vintage."

"Yeah, sure. If it makes you feel better, I'll wedge a chair under the doorknob."

"Can't you go to the Motel 6 on Fourth Street?"

"Maggie Bell, it's sweet that you're worried

about me. But I *am* a trained police officer. I've got this under control until I can get the landlord to fix the lock."

"I don't like it."

"There's not much we can do tonight. Go home. We'll talk in the morning."

"Keep your gun loaded and next to your bed," she warned.

"Always do," Gary replied.

He tapped the roof of her car, then disappeared back into his apartment.

Maggie pulled away, but she knew there was no chance she'd be sleeping anytime soon. Her nerves were buzzing. Fair Haven was quiet, the roads mostly empty except for a few late-night drivers heading to the gas station or liquor store.

She needed somewhere to burn off this adrenaline. A left, then a right, then straight for a few blocks. She followed the signs to the looming structure of St. Joseph Hospital.

Something was happening at the emergency entrance. People were crying, rushing, shouting.

Perfect.

She parked in a nearby lot and joined the small crowd heading inside. Now all she had to do was figure out which floor Agnes Krueger was on.

Chapter 16

I t wasn't that Maggie had to sneak in to see Agnes Krueger because she was under heavy guard or in some infectious disease unit requiring a hazmat suit. It was just that visiting hours were over.

The real challenge was finding out what room Agnes was in. Maggie didn't want to wait until morning. Her curiosity about the incident at Lora Foretree's house had reached full boil. Even if it meant sneaking into a hospital and waking up a potentially concussed patient, she needed answers.

"No need to be sneaky, Mags," she murmured to herself. "Just ask."

Summoning courage from the soles of her feet, Maggie approached a woman in purple scrubs by the front desk who wasn't occupied with the frantic crowd that had shuffled in all at once.

"Excuse me," Maggie said politely. "My sister was admitted earlier today. Her name's Agnes Krueger. Can I see her?"

The woman checked a gold watch snug around her plump wrist, then looked at Maggie, who tried to muster a few tears. The result was an awkward smile that made her look more like she was holding in gas.

"She's not in the ER anymore. They moved her to the fifth floor," the nurse said with a firm nod. "But visiting hours are over. You can see her first thing at six."

With that, the nurse turned back to assist the growing crowd. Judging by the bloody rags, limping gaits, and anguished cries, Maggie figured there'd been a serious accident, maybe a car crash. Whatever it was, it had everyone's attention, leaving Maggie free to slip away.

She ducked behind the desk and moved into the corridor connecting the emergency wing to the main hospital.

Once past the chaos, she entered the wide, quiet lobby of the main building. A few people were stretched out across vinyl chairs. A muted television played above them, closed captions rolling across the bottom of the screen.

Across the room stood a bank of elevators. A lone attendant manned the round information desk in the center of the space. Maggie kept one eye on the desk and the other on the elevators. She took a deep breath and walked briskly as if she knew exactly where she was going.

She pressed the "up" button, wincing at how loud it sounded in the hushed lobby. With her back to the information desk, she peeked over her shoulder.

Still unnoticed.

Was it really going to be this easy? She could've had a completely nefarious motive and no one would've stopped her. Here she was, about to roam a hospital unsupervised, surrounded by the sick, the elderly, and newborns, even. Didn't anyone care?

Just as she began silently ranting about the hospital's lack of security, the elevator chimed.

To Maggie, it sounded like a tornado siren.

She didn't dare turn around. Even when she heard the receptionist's voice call out.

"Miss? Excuse me! Where are you going?"

Maggie held her breath, silently praying the

elevator doors would open faster, or that the floor might swallow her whole.

"I'm going to see my sister," she muttered, barely above a whisper, as the doors slid open. No one stepped out. Good.

"What did you say? You need to come back here, miss. *Miss!*"

Maggie stepped into the elevator, pressed the button for the fifth floor, and begged the doors to close.

As they began sliding shut, she heard the screech of wheels, someone pushing a rolling chair, followed by rapid footsteps and the woman's increasingly irritated voice.

"Miss! Stop!"

Maggie finally turned. The receptionist was waddling toward her, arms flailing like propellers, determination etched on her face.

There was no way she'd reach the elevator in time.

Still, Maggie made a show of looking everywhere *but* at the woman, pretending she didn't see her.

Just before the doors sealed shut, their eyes locked.

Maggie felt the full force of the woman's irritation, and knew instantly this was going to make getting out of the hospital a lot harder.

"I'll worry about that when I'm done," Maggie whispered to the empty elevator.

When the door to the fifth floor opened, she squinted, half-expecting a SWAT team to be waiting for her like she was wired with explosives. But the hallway was empty. She stepped out and looked both ways.

The nurses' station was to the right. Two women in purple scrubs were focused on their charts. Neither looked up.

Quietly, Maggie tiptoed down the hall, peeking into rooms as she went. Some were completely dark. Others had the soft flicker of a television casting ghostly light. One room had a nightstand lamp turned on. If this wasn't Agnes Krueger's room and she disturbed the wrong patient, the whole thing would be over, and she'd once again be explaining to Gary how she'd wandered someplace she wasn't supposed to be.

She peeked inside.

"What in the world are you doing here?" Agnes snapped, sitting upright in a hospital gown, her arms marked with hospital wristbands.

Maggie slipped in and shut the door behind her.

"Risking life and limb. Gary... I mean, Officer Brookes told me what happened."

"You two sure are a cozy pair," Agnes said, arching her brow.

"We've known each other since high school."

"Oh, that explains it," Agnes rolled her eyes. "Still doesn't tell me what you're doing here. I don't think you're working with the guy who clobbered me. If you are, you're the tiniest assassin I've ever seen."

"It's nothing like that. I just wanted to know why you were at Lora's house. What were you looking for?"

"Who wants to know?"

"Me."

"What for? Wait, don't tell me. You're helping out your boyfriend in uniform because he's on thin ice with the commissioner, or the chief, or whatever cliché cop movie thing is going on. Willing to risk life and limb so he can crack the case," Agnes teased. "I told you. I'm going to solve this. And once I do, my business is going to explode. Big-name clients, coast to coast. Hollywood to D.C."

"All from solving one murder in Fair Haven, Connecticut? That's... ambitious," Maggie said, her tone dry.

This wasn't going how she'd hoped. If she didn't dial it back, Agnes would have her tossed out by security.

"You've got a smart mouth for someone who probably weighs eighty pounds soaking wet," Agnes growled. For a second, Maggie thought she might actually climb out of the bed, IV lines and all, and deliver a slap. But she stayed put.

Maggie held up her hands and looked down.

"I'm sorry. That came out wrong."

"You bet it did."

"I'm not here to argue. I just want to know what you saw at Lora's place. That's it."

Agnes sighed and looked up at the ceiling. After a moment, she turned back to Maggie.

"I didn't get as far as you did. The place was locked up tight. I was trying to figure out how to get inside without drawing attention. You really do have a gift for that sort of thing."

"Yup," Maggie replied, and stepped a little closer.

"Yeah, well, I couldn't crack it. I snuck around to the back porch, hoping to find a key hidden in one of those fake rocks or under a gnome or something. While I was searching, someone came up behind me. Next thing I knew, I was in some kind of chokehold."

"You mean a headlock," Maggie said. "A full Nelson would just pin your arms. This... this was more oxygen-deprivation-y."

Agnes grimaced. "You're weird."

"I get that a lot."

"All I know is, everything started to go dark. I couldn't fight back. He was behind me, and my stun gun was useless. I'd have zapped myself."

"Did you get a look at him?"

"Nope. All black. It wasn't completely dark out, but dark enough that I couldn't make out any features."

"You're sure it was a man?"

Maggie thought of the figure that had chased her to her front door. She had assumed it was a man, but like Agnes said, it was dark.

"Pretty sure," Agnes nodded. "Why?"

Maggie gave a quick explanation of her own experience. She shivered a little as she finished, and Agnes's expression softened.

"There really is more to you than meets the eye," she said. "You're like a trapdoor spider. No one sees you coming until it's too late."

"I've never jumped anyone. Or dragged them into a hole to inject venom and save them for a late-night feast," Maggie said. Realizing the room had fallen silent, she looked at Agnes, who was giving her a wary stare. "Sorry. Go on with your story."

Agnes shook her head. "As I was saying. The only reason I got out of that mess was because I've taken a few self-defense classes. I know I left some marks on the guy. And I had enough faith in this sleepy town to know the neighbors would be on high alert. I started screaming at the top of my lungs. I don't think he expected that. Wouldn't be surprised if every stray cat in Fair Haven came running." She chuckled.

"You're really brave," Maggie said.

"I don't know if it's bravery. Maybe just a healthy dose of recklessness. But I knew someone had to be watching that house after everything that happened with Lora Foretree." Agnes paused, stifling a yawn. "Sure enough, a couple of old-timers came out onto their back porch shouting, 'Hey! What's going on over there? We're calling the police!' I swear, it only took seconds before the cops showed up. They must've had the same feeling I did."

She rubbed her eyes and swallowed.

"I don't want to keep you up any longer than I have to," Maggie said.

"It's fine. I'm tired, but even when I turn out the lights, I won't be able to sleep. Hospitals are the worst for resting."

"You're sure it was just one guy?" Maggie pressed. She remembered the man who'd chased her at Mrs. Peacock's. And now the two shady guys from the hotel flashed through her mind. Gary hadn't said if they'd come forward. Maybe they played her, and maybe they were behind Agnes's attack.

"Positive. He was tall. Not a bodybuilder, not scrawny either. Just big in the sense that he towered over me. It's hard to describe a specter."

Maggie pictured Handy. He fit the height. But could he run that fast? Could he slip past Gary unnoticed? She doubted it. Crush was shorter, and definitely out of the question.

Agnes yawned again. "I'll tell you this much, Maggie. When I find him, he's giving me back my stun gun. And a pound of flesh."

Whether it was the late hour or maybe a sedative that dulled her edge, Agnes's eyes were heavy now. But she'd given Maggie more than she expected. Maybe more than she knew what to do with.

Now came the hard part: getting out.

An image formed in Maggie's mind of orderlies creeping through the corridors. One carried a baton. Another had one of those long poles with a loop at the end, like they used to catch gators in Florida. She'd be lassoed and tossed into a padded room, never to be seen again.

Shaking off the vision, she gathered her courage, crept to the door, and peeked into the hallway. Empty. The nurses were still softly chatting. The elevator was just past their station.

She moved as quickly and quietly as she could. The soft pat of her shoes was the only sound. She didn't glance at the nurses as she passed. At the elevator, she hit the button.

It dinged immediately. The doors slid open. Maggie stepped in, turned, and jabbed the "close" button like it might save her life.

"Who was that?" she heard one nurse say, just as the doors slid shut.

She exhaled deeply as the elevator carried her down.

The real challenge was still ahead. There was no way to exit the hospital without passing the information desk. If she got stopped, she'd stick to one story: she came to see Agnes Krueger, it was urgent, and now she was leaving. She wouldn't be back.

That was the plan.

She squared her shoulders, lifted her chin, and braced herself. When the elevator reached the lobby and the doors opened, Maggie saw the lumpy, middle-aged security guard at the desk. He was chatting with the same wide-hipped woman who'd chased her earlier.

"That woman. Right there," the woman pointed.

The guard lifted his hand in acknowledgment, but didn't move toward Maggie.

She looked at the sliding glass doors.

Then, in a sudden panic, she bolted. The doors opened slowly. To her, it felt like an eternity. In truth, maybe two seconds passed before she slipped through and into the night.

In her mind, she was as slick as a cat burglar.

In reality, she ran like a drunk toddler trying to escape her mom at a department store.

But it worked.

She made it to her car, started the engine, and drove away. A few blocks later, two police cruisers sped past her, lights off but moving fast, heading in the direction of the hospital.

She'd find out soon enough if they were coming for her. For now, she was just going home.

Chapter 17

"How did I know it was you snooping around the hospital?" Gary asked as he took the large coffee from The Bookish Café that Maggie had brought to the police station.

"Did I cause a lot of hoopla?"

"Not really. The security guard and front desk receptionist both confirmed it. No one reported any trouble on the floors. They just chalked it up to some weirdo sneaking in. Happens all the time," Gary said, prying off the lid and taking a careful sip. He let out a deep sigh. "Best coffee in town."

Maggie sat in the chair next to Gary's desk, hunching slightly to keep her voice low.

"Do you know who the officer was that

responded to Lora's house when Agnes was attacked?" she whispered.

"Yeah," Gary whispered back, leaning in.

"Who was it?"

"Me."

"Really? You didn't tell me that," Maggie huffed, sitting up straight.

"You didn't ask."

Maggie crossed her arms and clicked her tongue. The way Gary snickered made her cheeks flush. He was exactly the same as in high school. She'd be in a whirlwind over something—an exam, a missing book, a forgotten appointment—and Gary would be the one sitting there with all the answers. He'd casually tell her the test was Wednesday, not Tuesday. That her book was in his locker. That she'd written her notes on a Post-it instead of in her planner. It was like he enjoyed watching her squirm.

"Did you go into the house after Agnes was taken to the hospital?"

"No. It was locked up tight. Real tight," he replied, narrowing his eyes at her.

"We need to go inside."

"What for?"

"The killer went back there. He was looking for

something. I've seen the inside, and I might notice if something's missing or out of place. That's worth checking, don't you think?"

Gary leaned back and took another sip of coffee. "I hate to tell you this, Mags, but that's a great idea."

Maggie smiled and blushed. "Really?"

"Yeah. Oh, and since when do you know a couple of goons named Handy and Crush?"

Maggie's jaw dropped.

"So, you do know them. They stopped by late last night, but I was already asleep in the empty holding cell."

"Yeah, I know... Wait. You slept in the holding cell? Oh, Gary. That's pitiful. Why didn't you just come to my house?"

"First of all, you weren't home. You were busy sneaking around the hospital like the Grim Reaper looking for a low pulse. Second, it was cheaper than the Motel 6 on 4th Street. And you don't know what a good night's sleep is until you've been run ragged and crash in a six-by-six cell you've got the keys to. I slept like a baby."

Maggie squinted at him and tilted her head like a dog hearing a high-pitched noise. "I don't get you."

"You're not supposed to, Mags. I'm a mystery. An enigma." He smirked.

"A horse's aa—"

"That's enough," he cut her off, pointing a finger, which made her laugh.

"Let's saddle up, Roy. We've got some snooping to do."

Before long, Maggie and Gary were back at Lora Foretree's house. Yellow police tape surrounded the property. Nothing looked disturbed. All the ugly gnomes were still in place, keeping watch.

"Do you like those things?" Maggie asked as Gary parked the car.

"What things?"

"Garden gnomes."

"Haven't given them much thought. I live in an apartment."

"If you had a house, would you put those creepy little guys in your yard?"

"Probably not. Of course, now that I've said that, if I ever move into a house, I know what you'll be buying me as a housewarming gift." He chuckled.

"They're expensive. I'm not spending that kind of money on you," Maggie said, surveying the property. "They give me the creeps. Just ugly little things. You know they're watching us."

Gary shook his head and led the way to the back of the house. Police tape stretched across the entrance, along with a warning label stating that breaking it could lead to criminal trespass charges. Gary pulled out his pocketknife and sliced through the tape.

"You aren't going to get in trouble?" Maggie asked.

"Since when does getting in trouble bother you?"

"It's one thing for me to get in trouble. It's another to drag you into it."

"You aren't dragging me anywhere. Besides, I'm investigating this crime. I've got a job to do. You, on the other hand, are just an interloper. So act accordingly. Don't touch anything."

"I know," Maggie snapped in a whisper, as if even her voice might disturb the silence. The house smelled stale and stuffy. Gary pulled a couple of rubber gloves from his pocket and handed a pair to Maggie. With a tug and a snap, she slipped them on but clasped her hands behind her back and followed Gary carefully.

"Let's start upstairs and work our way down," Gary said.

"You mean upstairs, to the bathroom?"

"You were up there. You were the first one to see Lora dead."

"Second," Maggie whispered. "The killer saw her first."

With a solemn nod, Gary waved her on to follow him up the stairs. It was warmer on the second floor. The utilities had been shut off, and the hot air from downstairs had risen and settled in the hallway and rooms. The bathroom looked the same, minus the body in the tub. Blood still clung in dark patches to the porcelain and tiles. The shower curtain hadn't been removed.

"What are forensics waiting for?" Maggie asked, still whispering.

"They've already been here and took what they could. But the tub and curtain were wet. Nothing stuck. They'll toss those things once we're completely finished here. And why are you whispering?"

Maggie cleared her throat. "I guess I just don't want to disturb anything."

"I get it. So, do you see anything strange? Different? Out of place?"

Maggie looked around. She hadn't paid close attention to the bathroom on her first visit. Her focus had been entirely on the tub. Now, nothing looked different. Nothing had been rifled through. The spare room was untouched. The bedroom looked the same—until something caught her eye.

"Look at this," she said, pointing to the large mirror over the dresser. Pictures were tucked into the seam between the mirror and the frame. Maggie plucked one out. It showed a smiling Lora Foretree with a man's arms wrapped around her. Judging by the man's build, it wasn't Dane McKenny. That might explain why his head had been torn from the photo.

"Who do you think that is?" Gary asked.

"No idea. Could be from years ago. Maybe she just liked how she looked in this one. She does look good. Wow, would you look at that ring on his finger? There ought to be a rule against men wearing giant, gawdy costume jewelry. That thing looks like something Dracula would wear."

"You know those hardcore bikers. They wear jewelry that matches their bikes. Only a Harley guy could pull off a ring like that."

"Do you think he wears it all the time? Like to the grocery store? Or church?"

"I don't know, Mags." Gary chuckled.

"Do you think the killer tore his own face out of the photo? Maybe that's what he was doing when he came back."

"If that's the killer, I think he would've taken the whole picture, don't you?" Gary said, slipping the photo into a plastic baggie. It would be dusted for fingerprints.

"You're probably right. If he even knew it was here," Maggie said. "Still, that ring is practically a felony. You should be able to write a ticket for something that tacky."

They carefully made their way downstairs. Gary took out his flashlight and shined it along the stairs as they descended, slowly scanning each step.

"What are you looking for?" Maggie asked.

"Anything left behind."

Maggie nodded. Her eyes drifted to the walls, still covered in photos of Lora with her Harley-Davidson. She stepped into the living room and took a deep breath. It was slightly cooler on the main floor, but the air remained stale. The furniture looked untouched. The kitchen was just as she'd left it.

"How do you have an affair with someone with

a family who lives close by? Do you expect no one to notice? I don't get it," Maggie muttered.

"Unfortunately, it happens. I don't get it either. If you love someone enough to marry them, why would you look anywhere else? Or just get a divorce."

"Yeah."

"Yeah," Gary echoed. He looked at Maggie. "Too bad people aren't as smart as us. The world would be a better place."

Maggie wrinkled her nose and scanned the room before nodding. A few quiet minutes passed. Then, as if he'd been holding in the question, Gary cleared his throat.

"Mags?"

"Yeah?" she said, getting down on her hands and knees to peek under the sofa and armchairs. If Gary thought to check the stairs, snooping under the furniture wasn't out of the question.

"Do you ever think about getting married?"

She took a breath. "Sometimes."

"Would you have a big wedding or a little one?"

"You ask like you don't know me. I'd have a small wedding. That way, if the guy doesn't show, I won't have too many people to explain it to."

Gary chuckled. "You're not that pessimistic."

Maggie blushed. "No. But I'd still keep it small. How about you? If you can keep her hogtied long enough, would you get married and have a big wedding?"

"You're a real riot, you know that?" Gary said as he walked into the kitchen. "Yeah. I'd like to get married someday. I think I'd elope. Just her and me."

"To Vegas?"

"No. Just to a quiet little Justice of the Peace. A honeymoon overnight in a No-Tell Motel, then back home to announce I'm off the market."

Maggie followed him into the kitchen and gave him a teasing look. "Yeah. Someone finally found you in the discount bin."

Gary chuckled.

"I think that sounds nice."

"You do? I would've thought you'd say it was cheap or tacky," Gary said, opening the refrigerator and peeking inside.

Maggie stepped beside him to look as well. Inside were a few cans of Diet Coke, a tub of margarine, some questionable leftovers in Tupperware, and a lonely loaf of bread.

"Well, I do think those things," Maggie replied, "but I also think the right woman would find it perfect. It suits you. Besides, who else would protect Fair Haven in your absence? Crime doesn't take a vacation."

Gary was still smiling when he noticed Maggie had gone very still. Her gaze had locked on the kitchen table, and her eyes narrowed to little slits.

"What?" he asked.

She pointed. "The card. From Dane. It's gone. Did your guys take it?"

"What card?" Gary looked confused.

"There was a card sitting there. I saw it when... I snuck in," Maggie said, folding her arms. "It was made out to Peppermint. That was Lora's nickname from Dane. I told you, it was dated the same day I found her body. The killer must've come back to get it. I'll bet he was in the middle of it when Agnes Krueger showed up. You need to question Dane again. If you put the squeeze on him, he'll sing like a canary."

"Put the squeeze on him? What have you been reading?"

"Nothing, unfortunately. I've been too wrapped up in this mess to crack the binding on any of the new books for the café. Except for *Small Town Secrets*. I'm going to be honest, Gary, if I never hear another secret again in my life, it'll be too soon."

Gary ran a hand through his hair, then looked at the kitchen table, under it, around it, and finally let out a sigh.

"You're sure you saw it?"

"Yup. Saw the date. Saw the nickname. It was right there," Maggie said as she knelt to peek under the lower cabinets. Spotting the trash can, she daintily picked through it. "Nothing here that looks like anyone tossed it. Nope. If you go talk to Dane, I'm telling you. You'll find out he came in and took it. Because he's guilty."

"Maggie Bell, that's circumstantial at best."

"It puts Dane in the house on the day Lora was murdered. He was having an affair with her, but now he claims he loves his wife. Otto blew it all up. The most dangerous animal is the one backed into a corner. And Dane is in a pretty tight corner. Go talk to him. He'll crumble into a million little pieces."

"I don't think going to his place is the best idea. I'll tell him to come down to the station," Gary said as they made their way to the back door.

"Great. We can grill him there," Maggie said, striding ahead into the fresh air. All the garden gnomes stared as they exited the house.

"I love how you just invite yourself to things before anyone's even invited you," Gary said with a chuckle.

Chapter 18

It was quiet at the police station. It usually was in Fair Haven. People knew how to behave. They knew their neighbors. And now that someone who had written a book about their secrets had turned up dead, Maggie was sure most residents wanted to keep things peaceful.

She took a seat at Gary's desk and watched as he picked up the phone and cleared his throat.

"Hello, Dane?" Gary asked Dane to come to the station at his earliest convenience. "No, there was no problem. Just a couple of follow-up questions. Well, it really would be best if you came in today, but first thing tomorrow morning would be fine too."

Maggie leaned back, and shook her head. A

delay tactic. The guy was hiding something. Maybe he felt guilty or maybe he sensed the walls closing in. She wanted to urge Gary to insist he come in immediately. But all she heard Gary say was that he understood and yes, family came first.

If he'd actually put his family first, none of this would be happening, Maggie thought as she pinched her lips and looked at Gary, who smirked as he hung up.

"What's that look for?" he asked.

"He's not coming in?"

"Tomorrow morning. He's got plans with his family tonight," Gary said, waiting for Maggie's reaction. She didn't disappoint.

"Plans with his family. Don't make me laugh. If those plans fall through, what's to stop him from catching the next flight out of town?"

"Maggie, Dane McKenny isn't going to skip town."

"He might." She leaned forward. "Two people are dead. One was his mistress. The other exposed the affair. You're right. Skipping town is crazy talk. What am I thinking?"

"That sarcastic bone of yours is growing faster than the rest of you," Gary muttered. "Would it help if I promised to keep an eye on the McKenny estate until tomorrow?"

"I could do it for you," Maggie offered, eyes wide like someone had just told her Christmas was coming early.

"No. And if I see you within five blocks of that house, I'll have you arrested for trespassing."

"Gary, you wouldn't do that to me. After all we've been through."

"High school doesn't count."

Maggie pouted, but before she could reply, the front door of the station rattled open, and two familiar faces appeared.

She stood and crossed her arms. "I don't believe it," she muttered.

Handy and Crush paused, looking surprised to see her.

"We were gonna come sooner, but my mom got sick," Crush said, glancing at Maggie, then quickly looking away. "We came last night but it was too late."

"You didn't tell me your mom was sick," Handy mumbled, earning an elbow to the ribs.

"Tell it to the judge," Maggie said. She looked at Gary.

"So what's this all about about?" Gary asked, lowering his voice. He pulled over a chair and motioned for the guys to sit down.

Maggie, who wanted more than anything to stay and listen, was quietly told to go home.

"But I organized this. I found them. I've got questions too, like why it took them so long to show up," she said, squinting at the two.

"Stop giving them dirty looks and go home. I'll call you tonight," Gary said, gently turning her toward the door.

"Promise?" she asked, her gaze still fixed on the two men, who were now looking anywhere but at her.

"Yes, Mags."

"Bye, Maggie," Handy said as she passed. His voice softened her expression. As much as she wanted to scold them for the delay, there was something harmless about their tough guy routine.

When she stepped out of the station, the sky was a bright blue and the sun blinding. The scent of hot dogs from a nearby cart hit her like a dream.

Just what she needed.

She pulled a few dollars from her pocket, bought two dogs with mustard and a Coke, then found a bench to sit for a moment and enjoy her late lunch.

A trip to the bookstore was in order. She was back at work the next day. Vacation over. Sort of.

She still had a book signing to organize for Fifi, but that would be simple. A table, a chair, maybe some flowers. The Bookish Café already had copies of Fifi's book, plus any she brought herself should be more than enough.

She'd confirm the details once she got home, since Fifi was staying with Mrs. Peacock. Maggie wondered if Trent knew where Fifi was and whether he might be lurking nearby, hoping to corner her.

After another sip of Coke, Maggie stood and headed toward the bookstore.

What kept popping into her mind wasn't all the information she and Gary had gathered.

It was Gary. Her high school buddy. The one person she never felt awkward around. Lately, they'd been spending a lot of time together. And as she walked along the sidewalk in her usual quiet way, head lowered but eyes up, she realized something. She missed having him walk beside her.

"Snap out of it, Mags. You're just getting a little clingy. He's like a cousin, and this isn't the South," she muttered.

A man in a polo shirt and skinny jeans turned and gave her a look.

"Well, it isn't," she barked. He shrugged and kept walking.

With a squint, just as she pushed her glasses up, Maggie suddenly wondered about Gary's motives. Did he mind her always tagging along? If she hadn't, he wouldn't be nearly as far in the case as he was now.

How far is that, Mags? she thought, resisting the urge to mutter like a lunatic. He had a few suspects, no solid evidence, and had helped cover for her when she trespassed into the home of a murder victim no one knew was dead until she broke in.

"Well done, Mags," she muttered again, rolling her eyes as two teenage girls passed by, giggling.

But who else could she talk to about any of this? She'd been at the hotel when Otto was killed. She'd spoken to him. Seen the only fan he had. Witnessed how the entire town had turned its back on him for daring to write about the affairs, embezzling, and lies everyone knew were happening but no one wanted exposed.

All the ingredients of a good book, and she had a front row seat. She wanted Gary beside her for every chapter of it.

"You have a crush on him." The voice was loud. Clear.

"What? No, I don't!" Maggie practically shouted before realizing the voice belonged to a young woman chatting with a friend at the cross-walk. They both stared. Maggie swallowed, pushed her glasses higher, and hurried past.

No one is talking to you, she scolded herself. *But you sure have a lot to say to all of them.* What was wrong with her? She couldn't blame hunger. The weather was perfect. Maybe she needed a nap. Or maybe the truth was, she and Gary had always been more than just compatible. Something had kept them at arm's length, until now. Maggie had shifted the dynamic, and Gary didn't even real-ize it.

Now what was she supposed to do?

Without thinking, she stepped into the book-store and set her purse behind the counter.

"What are you doing here?" Joshua emerged from the café side with a steaming mug in hand.

"Oh, uh..." Maggie scratched her head, eyes dropping to her shoes. She was technically still on vacation, but the reason she came in popped into her mind. She snapped her fingers.

"I managed to get one of the authors from the convention to do a book signing here. Do you think tomorrow would be—"

"Serafina Lawson? Or did you snag someone else?" Joshua asked, taking a sip.

"No. Serafina Lawson is right. How do you know?"

"Mrs. Peacock called. Said you two had spoken, and she wanted to organize the event for her dear friend. She also offered to handle all the publicity." Joshua raised his brows. "Serafina will be here Thursday. According to your landlady, she's staying until every book is gone and promised to spill a little local tea while she's at it."

"How many books do we have?"

"Fifty in-store. Serafina's got another three hundred in her car. Let's hope Mrs. Peacock really gets the word out." He chuckled.

"She's already called Mrs. Donovan. I'd bet the news is halfway across town by now." Maggie crossed over to the window display she'd set up before her time off.

"Let's hope so. And for the record, your window display is getting lots of compliments again. But I don't think you'll win this month."

Maggie whipped her head around. "Why not?" She didn't expect to win every time, but anyone strolling down Main Street could see The Bookish Café had the best displays.

"The bank might have you beat."

"The bank? What did they do, tape dollar bills to the glass?" Maggie groaned. She hated going in there. The ladies at Fair Haven Bank were one step below Mrs. Peacock and Mrs. Donovan in the town gossip rankings, and all of them acted like Joshua was the last eligible bachelor on Earth. Normally, their décor amounted to flowerpots by the door.

"Nope. They had kindergarteners draw pictures of Fair Haven and posted them all over the windows. They're cute." Joshua shrugged.

"They're diabolical." Maggie clenched her fist, then sighed. "I know when I'm beat. Kindergarteners. You can't compete with a crayon-powered cuteness overload."

Joshua laughed, and Maggie couldn't help but smile.

"I think we should have Fifi in the chair at the back. It'll make a small crowd seem cozier, and if we get a big one, people can line up through the stacks," she said, pointing around the bookcases. "Your dad's little desk would be perfect for the signing station, don't you think?"

"I do," Joshua nodded.

"Fifi will love it. And Mrs. Peacock will love it

even more. She'll get all the bragging rights for pulling it off."

"So, you'll be here tomorrow?" Joshua asked.

"Yeah. Vacation's over."

"Good. I know you probably wanted a few more days off, but it's just not the same when you're not here." He smiled, then cleared his throat and headed back to the café.

"What did he mean by that?" Maggie muttered, nose wrinkled.

Chapter 19

Whate Maggie arrived at her home, the construction crew was still working on her driveway. She hadn't imagined the process would take so long. But when she saw only two workers—one operating the small digger and the other shouting directions—it made more sense. She drove down Mrs. Peacock's long driveway, pulled up where her car would be out of the way, and saw that Fifi's vehicle was still in the same spot.

As she got out of her Dodge Neon, she listened for the ladies' voices on the back patio. It was quiet. Just the drone of the digger and the foreman's occasional bellow, nothing else.

"That's going to be lovely to listen to all afternoon," Maggie muttered as she walked through Mrs. Peacock's garden toward the front door of her cottage. One of the workers gave her a wave. She raised her hand quickly in return, then focused on unlocking her deadbolt and making a swift escape from further interaction.

As soon as she shut the door behind her and slid the locks back into place, she rolled her eyes at herself.

"What is wrong with you? They're not lepers. Just guys doing their job and building you a nice new driveway. No need to be rude."

Maggie peeked out the window. She'd come a long way in confronting her introverted nature. Going to the book fair and meet-and-greet had been part of that effort. But old habits were stubborn. Suspicion and natural awkwardness still ranked high on her personality chart, and only conscious effort would help her shake the shyness.

Determined, she opened the door again, stepped outside, and surveyed the mess of torn-up gravel and dirt. The same worker who'd waved looked up at her. She squared her shoulders, lifted her chin, and gave him a tight smile along with an awkward OK sign. He smiled back.

Before a conversation could develop, Maggie

darted back into the house, shut the door, and locked it quickly. Proud of her progress, she strutted to the bathroom for a shower and changed into comfy clothes for what she hoped would be a quiet evening.

She should have known better. A little after seven, Maggie's phone rang.

"Hello?"

"What are you doing?" Gary asked. He sounded like he'd just run up a flight of stairs.

"Reading one of my new books. What are you doing?" She frowned, unsure if she wanted the answer, based on the tone of his voice.

"Have you eaten yet?"

"No."

"Good. Meet me at Lora Foretree's house. Park a block away and walk."

"Gary, please tell me you haven't become one of those weirdos who picnic at crime scenes."

There was a pause.

"I'm not even going to dignify that. Just hurry up. I got a tip. Dane's packing his truck. Looks like he's planning to run."

"I'm leaving now."

She slipped on her gym shoes, grabbed her wallet and keys, and dashed out the door. She could feel the eyes of the two workers tracking her as she bolted across the yard. Moments later, she was speeding toward the McKenny house.

When she arrived, she spotted Gary's cruiser parked a block from the entrance to the cul-de-sac. As soon as she pulled up behind him, he stepped out.

"Are we waiting for backup?" Maggie asked.

"No. He's not under arrest. We're just here to talk. Find out why he's packing up. Maybe ask if he has a one-way ticket to Mexico City."

"We?"

"Yes, Mags," Gary said as he opened the passenger door for her. "I want you there to observe, listen, and tell me what I might miss. I'll do all the talking."

"So, no good cop, bad cop?"

"No."

"Are you sure? I'll let you be the good cop."

Gary looked over at her as he climbed behind the wheel. "You as the bad cop? I can't think of anything more ridiculous. You'd never pull it off."

"I could so. I'd be the baddest cop you ever saw. You'd be terrified of me. We might not even be able to stay friends afterward," Maggie huffed.

"Why do you insist on telling stories we both know would never happen?"

"I'm just saying I have many sides, Gary. Some you've never seen."

Gary chuckled. "All right, straighten up. We've got work to do."

As they turned down the street, they spotted Dane packing a duffle bag and a backpack into the back seat of his truck. The bed of the truck held a few suitcases, boxes of clothes, gadgets, and a handful of cooking utensils.

His shoulders slumped the moment he saw the squad car. Gary tapped the siren briefly but didn't turn on the lights. He pulled in behind the truck, blocking it in completely.

"Remember what I said. You're observing, not interrogating."

"Got it," Maggie nodded. Now wasn't the time for jokes. A suspect tied to two murders was about to make a run for it.

Dane shoved his hands in his pockets and stared at the ground. Then he glanced at the neighbor's house before slowly approaching the cruiser. Gary was already out of the driver's seat when Maggie stepped out of the car and quietly closed the door behind her.

"What's going on, Dane?" Gary asked with a calm tone that barely hid his irritation.

"Hey, Gary. I was just about to call you."

"You were? From where?"

"Heather kicked me out. Told me to pack my things and get out. I'm heading to my mom's place until things cool off." He swallowed hard, his expression pitiful.

When he finally noticed Maggie, he gave a short nod, then turned his eyes to the ground again. Or the neighbor's house. Anywhere but Gary, who stood taller and wore a badge and a gun. Maggie had to admit, the uniform suited him.

"Where does your mom live?" Gary asked.

"Wisconsin."

Maggie's mouth fell open. Gary said what she was already thinking.

"You didn't think it might be helpful to inform the police before relocating?"

"I was going to," Dane replied quickly, his eyes wide as he nodded.

"Dane, two people are dead. I'm not saying you did it. But you can't just..."

"I didn't do it. I swear on my kids..."

Maggie cringed. She hated when people said that, whether in books or real life. Swearing on your kids meant nothing if you were already proven to be a liar. The words echoed in her head as she looked at the truck. No car seats. No toys. No sign he was planning to take his children to Wisconsin.

Gary kept writing in his notebook, jotting down Dane's mother's information. Maggie scanned the yard. The kids' toys had been moved into the garage. A few garbage bags were stacked in a corner. She couldn't tell if they held trash or personal belongings. Then she noticed a note taped to the garage door.

While Gary continued pressing Dane with questions about Lora and their affair, Maggie quietly slipped into the garage and peeled the note off the door.

It was a letter of apology to his wife. Poorly written, full of clichés and spelling errors. He used "to" when he meant "too." He didn't confess to killing Lora. She hadn't expected him to. The apology focused entirely on the affair.

It was the usual drivel: he'd made a mistake, he was sorry, he missed their life together, he remembered how excited they were when the kids were born. It reeked of regret over getting caught, not over the betrayal itself. Still, there was something sad about it. He sounded like a man clinging to the last thread of a life already unraveling.

Maggie placed the note back on the door and quietly slipped out the way she came. She wasn't sure if Dane had even noticed her brief absence. If she were being questioned by the police about a murder, she might not notice small things either.

"If you know what's good for you, Dane, don't do this. If what you're telling me is true, then go hole up in a motel for a few nights. Your problem is that your alibi is dead," Gary said.

"Gary, why would I kill the only person who could clear me?"

"Because she contributed to the breakdown of your marriage."

"Lora and I were just a fling. Call it a midlife crisis or something. I don't know. All I can tell you is I love my wife and kids." Dane's voice cracked and, to Maggie's dismay, he began to cry.

She rolled her eyes and cleared her throat, not bothering to hide her disgust. Dane must've seen it, because he glared at her through watery eyes.

"It's true! You might not believe me, but it is! I'd give anything to take it back. I wouldn't have helped Lora with her basement if I knew it would ruin my marriage!"

Now he was sobbing in the middle of his driveway. Maggie squinted at him like he was a strange bug she couldn't identify.

"If your family means that much to you, Dane, then you need to stay and face this," Gary said. "You can't run off to your mother's house and expect the town not to assume you're guilty of two murders on top of cheating. What better way to prove to your wife you deserve another chance than to take the judgment and own what you did?"

Maggie was impressed. Gary's calm reasoning struck the right chord. Dane wiped his eyes and sniffled, nodding slowly. He promised to stay in town and said he'd go to the motel on 4th Street, the same one Maggie had once suggested Gary stay in after his place was broken into.

She snapped her fingers. "Mr. McKenny? Can I ask you one more question?"

He looked up, resigned. "Yeah."

"Can you confirm where you were last night?"

"I was here," he said with a sniff.

"Alone?"

"Sort of."

"Sort of?" she asked, gently this time.

"I was on the phone with my mom from around eight to maybe nine-thirty or ten. Maybe later.

Then my brother came by around eleven. I was feeling pretty low, and Mom got worried I'd do something stupid. So, she sent Reuben over to check on me. He lives in Kachetaw County. Why?"

"Would your mom and brother confirm that?"

"Yeah, of course. Why? Did someone else get killed?"

He looked at her like a scared Basset hound, genuinely afraid he might be accused of another crime.

"No, nothing like that," Maggie replied, then glanced back at Gary to let him take over.

Gary gave Dane a final few words of encouragement, and a lightly veiled warning not to leave town under any circumstances. If Dane was innocent, Gary assured him, the truth would come out eventually.

"I hope you're right. I just wish none of this had ever happened. After Heather had the kids, she barely noticed me anymore. It'd been so long since anyone looked at me like I mattered," Dane confessed to Gary, completely ignoring Maggie's presence.

Whatever shred of sympathy Maggie had felt evaporated instantly. She wrinkled her nose like something sour had just entered the air. Gary noticed and moved quickly to wrap things up. Before Maggie could say anything snarky, he ushered her back into the cruiser and drove her around the corner to her car.

"Did you hear that sob story? Poor guy didn't feel like a stud anymore once his wife had babies. Ugh. How cliché can you get?" Maggie groaned.

"That's what causes a lot of affairs. Sometimes it ends in divorce. Sometimes the couple works through it and comes out stronger. Murder usually isn't the outcome. Usually." Gary glanced over. "Why did you ask about his whereabouts last night?"

"You forgot? Your apartment was broken into," Maggie said, arching a brow over the rim of her glasses.

"Oh. Right. I don't think it was Dane."

"Me neither. The guy I saw climbing out of your bathroom window was a lot thinner. Maybe taller too. He was dressed all in black, so I might be a little off, but not by much."

"No. Not likely," Gary agreed. He dropped her at her car and told her to head back home.

"Where are you going?" she asked.

"To grab something to eat."

"Can't I come? You're the one who dragged me out of the house."

"Yeah, and that's why I figured you wouldn't want to sit in a diner dressed like that."

Maggie looked down and winced. She'd rushed out so fast, she was still wearing her oldest, comfiest clothes, the ones that added more wrinkles and folds to her figure than the face of an English bulldog.

Chapter 20

Within twenty minutes of getting back to her cottage and cutting through Mrs. Peacock's garden, Maggie was seated in her kitchen with Gary, both of them going over everything they'd learned over burgers. That included a debriefing on Handy and Crush, who had come to clear their consciences under pressure from a certain small, glasses-wearing bully who threatened to turn them in if they didn't.

"They actually called me a small, glasses-wearing bully?" Maggie asked around a mouthful of burger. Gary had brought her dinner: a fully loaded burger and fries with a chocolate milkshake. He'd gone for a double order of loaded cheddar fries and a Coke himself.

"Sure did," Gary replied, wiping his mouth with a napkin. "They were even worried you'd come back to the station. Said they didn't want to deal with you."

Maggie sat quietly, chewing slowly as she mulled over everything they'd uncovered so far.

"So, you think they're clear? No involvement?"

"Yup. But I'd still like to question the woman they were spying for. Problem is... I think she's dead."

"What?" Maggie blinked.

"Lora Foretree. I think she's the one who sent them. Her reputation took a nosedive after Otto's book. She had just as much motive to kill him as Dane did."

Maggie stared at the kitchen table, eyes narrowing. "Wait a minute..."

Gary paused, watching her face. "What is it?"

"A wig."

"What?"

"A wig! She was wearing a wig! Don't you see? She was there. Both times! At the book fair, when Dane swooped in and knocked Otto's books over, and again at the meet-and-greet! She was there, Gary! But in a wig. That's why her hair looked so poofy. Same body, same tan, but she didn't talk to anyone. She helped Otto with the books and talked to him at the bar later that night. I can't believe I missed it. It was Lora Foretree at both events!"

Maggie clapped her hands and bounced a little in her seat. She puffed out her chest, grinned, and took an enthusiastic bite of her burger.

"She's dead, Mags," Gary said gently.

Her shoulders slumped. She kept chewing. "Thanks for raining on my parade with one tiny, inconvenient fact."

"Glad to be of service," Gary said, smirking.

"But why would she sneak around in a wig? Why not just go as herself? Dane wasn't hiding anything, he made a whole scene at the book fair. Did he even realize that was Lora standing there in a wig?"

"When I first talked to him, and again with you today, I didn't get the sense he was holding anything back. A detail like Lora going after Otto in disguise would've come up. Even if just in bits and pieces."

"Unless he's some kind of criminal mastermind who knows how to hide his feelings," Maggie said, eyeing her fries.

"He's not. He was a cheater, not a mastermind. The kind of guy who doesn't realize what he's got until it's gone. That kind of man can be dangerous, sure, because he's got nothing to lose. But..."

"But what?"

Gary exhaled. "But I don't think he did it."

"I don't think so either. Still, something keeps nagging at me. He lied to his wife for ages. He doesn't have solid alibis for when Otto or Lora died. And he had motive, maybe even desperation. Plus, that card. 'Peppermint.'" She shuddered. "I don't even want to know how that pet name came about."

"Only you saw that card. It wasn't there when we looked around, remember?" Gary reminded her.

"Right. Like a storm cloud following me around, raining on any potential joy. Thanks, Gary," Maggie huffed.

Gary chuckled and glanced at her, his gaze lingering a little longer than usual. Maggie felt the heat rise in her cheeks.

"What?" she snapped.

"You're really funny sometimes," he said, like it was something he'd been meaning to admit but was unsure how it'd land.

"So are you. You ever notice that when you look

in the mirror?" she said flatly, then squinted at him over the rim of her glasses.

"Very funny. Honestly, I don't get why your phone isn't ringing off the hook with guys asking you out. What's wrong with the fellas in Fair Haven?"

"They probably see me with you all the time and assume we're a thing. Let's face it, we're always hanging out. You've known me longer than anyone. I don't feel like an awkward nerd around you, probably because you're nerdier than me, and that's saying something."

Gary grinned. "I gotta ask you, Mags. What do you think about Joshua Whitfield?"

Maggie paused mid-chew. She wasn't sure what Gary expected her to say. Did he want the truth? That she thought Joshua was dreamy and that he'd been unusually kind lately? Of course, maybe he was just being polite. A guy like him could have his pick of half the town, and most of the women made it obvious they were interested. Still, it seemed to Maggie like he was too focused on the café and bookstore to notice.

"He's a good boss?" she said, eyebrows high with faux innocence.

"That's not what I meant."

"I don't know, Gary. He's my boss, he's good with a hammer, and... well, I mean... you know. Why are you asking?"

Gary took a sip of his Coke and cleared his throat. "I just notice how he looks at you sometimes. Thought I'd ask. You know, asking for a friend." He smirked.

"I don't know what you're talking about. He doesn't look at me like anything. Maybe like a harmless bug that might land on his shirt. Plus, every single woman in town is barking up his tree. And I don't even think he reads the books we sell. That's just weird." She pushed her plate slightly away.

"Hey, you don't need to explain. I was just making conversation."

"A pretty intrusive kind of conversation."

"Since when has that stopped me?"

"Apparently not recently," Maggie muttered, rolling her eyes.

Gary leaned forward, suddenly serious. "I worry about you, Mags. There might come a time when I'm not around, and I need to know you've got someone looking out for you."

Maggie stared at him. "What does that mean?" Her voice was barely above a whisper.

"Nothing dramatic. Just that someday I might get married, or get transferred, or decide to live off the grid in a shack, selling pelts and rescuing lost hikers. If that happens, I won't be around to keep you in line."

"So, you're not dying? Not planning to get shot or anything?"

"No! Why would you even say that?"

"I'm just checking. Look, if you head off to parts unknown, that's fine. But don't act like I can't function on my own. I'm not some charity case. I'm just... weird," Maggie said, folding her arms as her temper simmered.

"That's not what I meant. I'm sorry. It didn't come out the way I wanted it to. Is it so wrong for a friend to worry?"

Maggie was quiet for a beat. "No," she said at last, letting her shoulders relax.

She glanced at the clock, and, as if reading her mind, Gary wiped his mouth, tucked their trash into the takeout bag, and stood up.

"I hate to run, but I've got paperwork to catch up on. Thanks for coming with me to talk to Dane."

"Yeah. Happy to help," she muttered, still unsure what to make of their conversation.

After walking him to the door and locking it behind him, Maggie returned to the kitchen and sipped the last of her chocolate milkshake, staring into space. What was Gary's motive? Was he fishing for info on Joshua, or on behalf of himself?

It was too much to sort out. She still had to prep for her return to work tomorrow and finish planning Fifi's book signing. Maggie exhaled deeply. Somehow, she felt like she hadn't had a vacation at all.

Chapter 21

Mrs. Peacock made good on her promise to handle all the publicity for her friend Serafina Lawson's book signing. Flyers were printed and posted all over town, and the local radio station encouraged listeners to stop by for a coffee, pick up a book, and meet one of Fair Haven's very own authors before she continued her book tour. Goodie bags were assembled for the first twenty-five customers, each one filled with a blank journal, a coupon for a free coffee or pastry, and an elegant writing pen.

"This is a cute idea," Maggie said to Mrs. Peacock as she peeked inside the bags displayed behind the signing station.

"Well, it's set me back a pretty penny. I'll have to eat very lightly the next couple of weeks to save that money back up. But it was worth it, don't you think?" Mrs. Peacock replied with a satisfied smile. She was dressed in a stunning lilac muumuu with swirling red flowers and elegant wedge heels that framed her bright red toenails.

"Yes, ma'am," Maggie said, pushing her glasses up her nose.

A small line of people had already formed outside the café just as Fifi arrived. It was a few minutes before nine, and she was as lively and excited as could be. Maggie thought she looked even more thrilled than she had at the convention or the meet-and-greet. Fifi strolled along the line, smiling, chatting, and posing for quick photos with the waiting fans.

When she stepped inside, flanked by Trent on one side and the ever-stoic Mr. Thomas James on the other, she scanned the bookstore, then waved wildly the moment she spotted Mrs. Peacock and Maggie. As always, she was dressed to impress, this time in a tight denim corset top, a long denim skirt that just barely concealed her matching stiletto boots.

"What a great place! You nailed it, Vivian!" Fifi swept in and hugged her friend tightly.

"It was my pleasure. I hope you have a hugely successful signing," Mrs. Peacock said. "Judging by the crowd, it looks like you've got plenty of fans in your hometown."

"I think I saw Mrs. Donovan out there," Fifi whispered.

"Well, it wouldn't be proper to pull her to the front of the line. She'll just have to wait her turn," Mrs. Peacock replied smoothly. Maggie was certain she caught a mischievous glint in her eye. The kind that said she'd very much enjoy watching Mrs. Donovan stew.

"Of course, it wouldn't," Fifi purred.

When she turned to Maggie, her smile widened again and she extended her arms. "Hello, darlin'. This is such a lovely space you've given me. Thank you so much."

"It's really Joshua Whitfield's place. I just work here," Maggie replied with an awkward smile as Fifi linked her arm through hers.

"Do me a favor," Fifi said in a confidential tone. "Find a seat at the other end of the café for Mr. Trent. He thinks he's going to latch onto my coattails and tag along to Virginia, where Mr. James and I are headed. Can you handle that?"

"Sure. Do you want me to ask him to leave altogether?" Maggie asked, giving him a quick sideways glance and secretly hoping for the opportunity to toss someone out of the bookstore.

Trent and Mr. James had hung back while Fifi chatted. Despite the fact that Thomas James, another local author from the convention, had to be at least two decades older than Trent, the two shared a similar build. Tall, thin, though Mr. James had a little more padding around the waist.

"No. The poor dear is severely smitten. I can't help it that some people take an act of kindness as an invitation to sink their claws in. I'll let him down easy. I've had to do it a million times before," Fifi tittered.

Maggie's eyes popped. "A million?"

"Well, maybe not a million. Maybe just two or three times," she giggled, patting her hair into place. It was clear she was no stranger to male attention. But unlike Maggie, Fifi knew exactly how to handle it, and how to stay in control.

"What about Mr. James?" Maggie asked.

"Mr. James is a different story. We're discussing a collaboration soon on a crime that took place not far from Fair Haven in the 1800s. My stories may be fiction, but no one can say I don't know my history," she winked.

"Oh. That sounds interesting."

"Yes. Mr. James has some delectable stories swirling around in that head of his. Why, just last night, he told me the tale of poor Otto Deitz's demise would make a marvelous read for spooky fall nights."

"It's a little soon for that, don't you think?" Maggie asked.

"Early bird gets the worm, honey. I think poor Mr. Deitz would be thrilled his fellow Fair Haveners followed his lead and found juicy stories in their own backyard," she winked again, her long lashes practically waving to Maggie, who couldn't help but smile.

Within minutes of opening, The Bookish Café was swarming with people. Joshua stood at the door greeting customers and encouraging them to grab a coffee or hop in line for an autograph.

"Or feel free to roam around and find your next page-turner," he called out.

Fifi was as gracious as Melanie Wilkes from *Gone with the Wind*, speaking sweetly and confidently to everyone as if they were long-lost friends. There wasn't a sour face in sight. Fifi could melt even the crustiest patron with a simple hello. She took her time chatting, laughing, telling stories, and listening with genuine interest as fans gushed about her books.

Maggie, thoroughly enjoying the event, began plotting ways to bring more authors in for future signings.

Across the room, poor Mr. Trent sat sulking in a chair, just like at the meet-and-greet. A steaming coffee sat untouched in his hand as he gazed mournfully at Fifi. Maggie, who wasn't used to approaching strangers, decided to check on the pitiful, love-struck fellow. She knew too well the sting of being ignored at social gatherings.

Pulling together a bit of courage and brushing aside her own awkwardness, she approached him. Squinting slightly like she needed bifocals, lifted her chin, and smiled.

"Trent, can I get you anything? We've got some great muffins, and Babs makes the best chocolate chip cookies."

He crossed one leg over the other, eyes still on Fifi. "I'm fine. Thank you." His coffee remained untouched, and he barely spared Maggie a glance.

Maggie straightened, smoothed her skirt, and

happened to catch Joshua watching her from the doorway. He grinned. She walked over and looked up at him, no squinting, no wrinkled nose.

"Something to say, boss?" she muttered.

"Don't call me that. You practically run this place. I'm just the fix-it guy by comparison."

"You pay the bills. And my paycheck. You're the boss," she said with a salute.

"Come on. That makes it sound like we aren't friends. We're friends, right?"

Maggie blushed. "Yeah. Yes, we're friends. Yes." She quickly looked around the room, eager to focus on anything other than Joshua, who was clearly enjoying her awkwardness more than a slice of apple pie.

Mmm... apple pie sounds good, she suddenly thought.

She looked over at Mr. Thomas James who, stoic as ever, was sitting in a high-backed chair just out of the sunlight, occasionally glancing up from his newspaper to scan the room before returning to the news. When he lifted the paper in front of his face, she saw it. The ring. The Dracula ring. She blinked, squinted, and leaned in for a better look.

"What are you staring at?" Joshua asked.

"He's wearing the ring," she whispered,

clutching his arm to pull him closer. "He's wearing the Dracula ring."

"What are you talking about?" Joshua asked.

"When Gary and I went back to Lora Foretree's house after Agnes got attacked, we saw a picture of Lora with a man wearing that ring. But his head was missing from the photo."

"What?"

"He's wearing the Dracula ring," she hissed again.

"So... are you saying that man is Dracula?"

Maggie looked up at him, unimpressed. "No."

"Because I thought vampires couldn't come out in daylight."

"They can't."

"So he can't be a vampire. Let alone *the* Dracula."

"I know that. What I'm saying is—"

"Are you drunk?"

"I wish. No. I need to call Gary. He'll know what to do."

"Gary Brookes?"

"Yes. Officer Brookes. He needs to get here. Fast."

She turned to head for the phone in Joshua's office nook, but a firm hand closed around her forearm. Her heart jumped. She looked up at him, eyebrows raised.

Mr. James hadn't been questioned. He hadn't mentioned knowing either murder victim. And now he was planning to *leave town with Fifi?* Every red flag in Maggie's brain was waving furiously.

"Maggie, you are not calling 9-1-1," Joshua said.

"Fine. I'll call his cell. But this *is* an emergency."

"You can't have the police show up here right now. We're already close to capacity. If people panic, it could get dangerous."

"Okay, okay. I'll call his cell and leave a message. He'll call back."

"I don't think I have his number in my Rolodex."

"That's fine. I know it by heart."

Joshua straightened. "You know his number by heart?"

"Of course. We've been friends since high school. He's going to faint when he hears what I've got to tell him."

Maggie walked toward the phone, but paused. Why had Joshua asked so many questions about Gary's number? Sure, it made sense not to cause a panic. But was that all it was?

Of course he's surprised. Because he likes you. Her conscience was suddenly smug. *No guy asks that unless he's at least a little interested.*

"Margaret," Mrs. Peacock called out just as Maggie reached for the phone.

"I'll be right with you, Mrs. Peacock."

"Sorry, dear. This is important."

"Just a sec—"

"Margaret. Would you be a princess and bring that velvet chair over to Fifi's table? My feet are killing me."

"Yes, Mrs. Peacock. Just give me one minute—"

"Oh look, Mrs. Donovan's finally made it up in line. Wearing those garish red shoes. Doesn't she know how ridiculous they look? Oh, Maggie. Let's get that chair right now. I really need to sit."

Maggie sighed and put down the phone. Mrs. Peacock was going to keep buzzing in her ear until she got her way. Maggie should've told her to wait, but Margaret Bell had been raised to respect her elders.

She dragged the velvet chair across the store with a clatter, plunking it down where Mrs. Peacock gestured. It wasn't center stage, of course, but it was still in full view of the signing crowd. Which, Maggie realized, was *exactly* the point.

This wasn't about comfort. It was about optics. Specifically, about Mrs. Donovan seeing Vivian Peacock seated beside the town's bestselling author, acting like royalty.

It irritated Maggie, but not enough to distract her. She stole a glance at Mr. James, who she *thought* was peeking out from behind his paper. Hard to tell, but it didn't matter. She was calling in the cavalry.

He had been questioned and released without ever mentioning he knew *both* victims. That omission screamed guilt.

She dialed Gary's number and left a message:

"You have to get here before the signing ends. He's leaving soon and he's going with Fifi. She might be in danger too. Please, Gary. Hurry."

The morning dragged on. By the time the line thinned, it was after three. Still no Gary. Every time the bell above the café door jingled, Maggie's heart leapt, only to crash again when it wasn't him.

"Where could he be?" she kept muttering as she rang up customers, stacked books, and fetched water and napkins for both Fifi and Mrs. Peacock. Gary might miss this opportunity.

Worse yet, Mr. James had noticed her watching him.

She could feel it. Every few seconds she was

glancing at him, then the door, then her watch, then him again. Either he knew she suspected him, or he thought she was flirting.

Either way, her stomach was buzzing.

Then the worst happened.

Chapter 22

"It's been such a wonderful time. I'm so grateful for everything you did to make today such a smashing success," Fifi said as she hugged Maggie.

Maggie had come to adore Serafina Lawson, but her response was stiff and distracted because she was still watching the door. She had to stall her just long enough for Gary to show up.

"Do you really have to leave today? Maybe stay one more day, host a quick workshop or something?" Maggie said, floundering.

"I'd love nothing better. But I'm driving Mr. James for a bit and, like I said, we're both headed to Virginia. We've got a plot to hammer out along the way." She winked.

"What about Trent?" Maggie asked, feeling as hopeless as the lovestruck gent himself.

"Oh. Right. I'd better handle that now," Fifi sighed. "Would you do me a favor and take these things to my car? It's unlocked. I parked just outside the alley on the south side. Just toss them in the trunk."

Maggie took Fifi's purse and a handled paper bag with the six unsigned copies of her book. Normally, she'd be thrilled the event was such a hit, but one person still hadn't shown, and she was desperate for it. Where was Gary?

She made her way through the back of the store and out into the alley. Turning right, she spotted the red car just where Fifi had said. She popped the trunk and hoisted it open, but froze.

Peeking out from a man's leather briefcase, overstuffed with notebooks, a manuscript, the butt of a stun gun, and yesterday's newspaper, was the card Maggie had seen on Lora Foretree's kitchen table.

Her stomach dropped. Her worst fear was confirmed. Mr. Thomas James was definitely connected to Lora Foretree.

"Are you done loading Serafina's car?" came the low voice behind her.

Maggie's mouth went dry. She stopped breathing. The shadow of Mr. James loomed behind her. He rested a hand on the hood and angled his body to block her from slipping past.

Her eyes darted toward the street. Too far. No one could see her from here.

"Uh. Yeah. Could you shut the trunk while I just—" She tried to edge past him, but he stretched out his arm and knocked her back against the car.

"Get in," he growled.

"What? Get in *where*?"

"Get in the trunk."

"No. Nope. I'm not getting in the trunk." Her voice cracked. "You killed Lora, didn't you? And Otto? Because... why?"

"I said get in the trunk," he hissed through clenched teeth.

"You think you can just kidnap me? I'm going to kick and scream and Fifi will hear me. If I'll get in the trunk, you can explain to her why you've got the bookstore clerk tied up in the back." She babbled, trying to stall. Her thoughts were scrambled, her hands slick with sweat, her heart pounding. But she forced herself to sound composed. She had to *look* like she had a plan. Maybe she'd get the chance to run.

Where the heck was Gary?

"Get in the trunk and lie down. You won't be making any noise," Mr. James said, pulling a cord from his jacket pocket.

She didn't need to look to know what it was. The same kind of cord that left marks on Otto's and Lora's necks. He did it. He killed them. But why?

"You're trying to figure it out," he said, his voice suddenly soft. The way he might have spoken to Lora. That explained no signs of break-in at her house. She knew Thomas James. They rode Harleys together. Maggie was starting to feel sick to her stomach.

Maggie's stomach churned.

"Yeah," she whispered. Her knees felt weak. She was either going to faint or puke. She bit her tongue hard. The sting snapped her back. The pain roused her enough to stiffen her muscles. She looked down, half expecting to see the pair of feet she'd seen the other day sticking out from beneath her Dodge. Her second encounter with Handy and Crush. Her heart jumped. That was it!

Without thinking, she crumpled to the ground and scrambled halfway beneath Fifi's car. But before she could get far, Mr. James's hand clamped around her ankle.

She grabbed the first grimy piece of undercarriage she could reach and held on tight.

Mr. James yanked and pulled, growling at Maggie to let go. She screamed *no* over and over, calling for help, though she knew the chances of anyone hearing her were slim. Her voice wouldn't carry from beneath a car. She could only pray she could hold on until someone, anyone, came to check on her. But the pain in her fingers was getting worse. Mr. James's grip wasn't letting up. With each yank, she was sure she'd be ripped free.

Then, just when she thought the next tug would be the end, Mr. Thomas James crumpled onto her legs.

At first, Maggie panicked, thinking he was crawling under the car with her to strangle her right then and there. She kicked and screamed and scrambled out the other end, coming up beside the front headlight. Through the windshield, she saw who had come to her rescue.

Agnes Krueger stood above him, a new stun gun in hand and a smirk on her lips.

"I knew it!" she shouted, pulling a couple of

zip-ties from her pocket. "This guy thought he was slick. His creepy coolness didn't fool me. Roll over, you piece of—"

Maggie staggered to the back of the car and stared at Mr. James. He looked stunned in more ways than one. His eyes were wide. A scrape marked the side of his forehead, probably from hitting the concrete. Agnes wasted no time. She zip-tied his wrists behind his back, then did the same to his ankles.

"I am really glad to see you," Maggie said, out of breath. "I tried calling Gary to come and question him and—"

"Gary was in a car accident," Agnes said flatly.

"What?"

"Yeah. I heard it on the scanner about three hours ago," she said while rolling Mr. James onto his side. Just then, a squad car pulled up behind them. Maggie didn't recognize the deputy at first, but she knew him by face. Fair Haven's police force wasn't big. Everyone lived in town, and instead of six degrees of separation, it was more like three.

Still, it wasn't Gary getting out of that squad car.

Without waiting, Maggie ran back into the

bookstore, trying to hold herself together. She found Joshua laughing with Fifi and Mrs. Peacock.

When they saw her face, the conversation stopped cold.

"Mags. What's wrong?" Joshua asked, concern rushing into his voice.

"Gary's been in a car accident. I've got to go to the hospital," she said, swallowing hard and biting her tongue to keep from crying. She was terrified that if she started, she wouldn't be able to stop. How could she drive like that? "And the police are arresting Mr. James out back," she added, jerking her thumb over her shoulder.

Suddenly there were a lot of questions flying around. Maggie looked at Joshua and, without a word, hurried to grab her purse and keys from underneath the register where she'd always kept them.

"I'll drive you," Joshua said.

"I'm okay," she replied.

"You look like you're about to lose it. Let me drive."

"I'm fine. Just let me go," she insisted. What was the big deal? She knew where the hospital was. She knew the route and the entrance to the ER. She'd just snuck in there the other night. Gary would probably find it funny that she was returning for him this time. Yes, he'd laugh at that.

Her eyes started to burn, but she blinked the tears back and handed her keys to Joshua. In minutes, they were in her car, speeding toward the hospital.

Thankfully, Joshua did all the talking to the nurses in the emergency room. No one looked familiar at this hour. The night shift employees that might remember seeing her probably wouldn't arrive for a couple more hours. She'd be on her way home by then. Gary would be fine. Maybe they'd keep him overnight, just to be safe. But he'd be fine.

"He's in surgery," the nurse said, handing them a visitor pass for the third floor. They were directed to a waiting area.

Maggie dropped into a chair and stared at the TV on mute.

"He'll be okay," Joshua said gently. "Probably nothing serious."

Maggie wanted to believe him. She wanted to relax into the warmth of Joshua's arm and the calming scent of his cologne. But she couldn't. She just nodded, pretending to listen so he wouldn't think she was ignoring him.

Then the doctor emerged. He was a serious looking man with a gray mustache and tortoise shell glasses.

"Are you here for Gary Brookes?" he asked.

Maggie only heard the first three words before she broke down.

Chapter 23

"Look at this," Maggie said. It had been two days since Thomas James had tried to kidnap and kill her. She sat beside Gary's hospital bed, pointing to the newspaper.

"What is it?" Gary croaked. He was sitting up for the first time since surgery. The bones in his left ankle had been nearly shattered, but the doctor predicted a full recovery after a few more procedures and physical therapy. With one broken rib and a badly strained wrist, he was still looking at another day flat on his back before going home.

"The write-up in the paper about Mr. Thomas James," Maggie huffed.

"What about it?"

"Get this: 'Rookie Private Detective Solves

Double Murder.' Are you kidding me?" Maggie snorted like a bull seeing red.

"Calm down," Gary said.

"*Agnes Krueger of AG Investigations took on another role that should have been the job of local authorities, catching a vicious killer who had already claimed two lives.*' Are they serious? You had just as much to do with solving those murders as she did. I don't see your name anywhere. And I certainly don't see mine. Oh, wait, here I am. *'Potential victim number three.'* Potential number three, Gary!"

"Better than being number two," Gary said, chuckling until the pain from his rib made him wince and grab his side.

Maggie pointed at him. "That's what you get for not taking this seriously. She was going to take the credit no matter what."

"It doesn't matter who gets the credit, Mags. The bad guy's caught. But I'll tell you this. If I ever decide to date seriously, I think I'll find someone from another town. Maybe even another state."

"Yeah. There are plenty of blind women out there," she teased.

Gary laughed again, then groaned. "Don't make me laugh."

"You might be right. Thomas James grew up

here in Fair Haven, met Lora Foretree at a biker rally a town over when she was taking a break from Dane McKenny. They had a fling, but when she broke it off to get back with Dane, he cooked up the most dramatic revenge plot imaginable. It could have been a book all on its own."

Gary tried to shift himself up and grunted as his rib, ankle, and wrist all protested. Maggie stood and tucked an extra pillow behind his head.

"I wonder what James would've done if Otto Deitz hadn't become the most hated man in Fair Haven after *Small Town Secrets*. It was easy to pin the murder on Dane McKenny. The circumstantial evidence was enough to press charges, maybe not enough to convict. But he's going to have a hard enough time bouncing back from this, even after being cleared of murder. He still cheated on his wife," Maggie babbled on. "It did look like Dane killed Otto and then Lora. Lora keeping secrets ended up being her downfall. If she'd told someone about her fling with Mr. James, and then turned up dead, you would've gone after him first."

"If I didn't, you would've."

"Yeah. Potential number three," Maggie muttered, tossing the newspaper aside.

Gary chuckled and groaned. "Stop being funny, Maggie. It hurts."

"Serves you right for making me worry. I wonder what Heather and Paige are doing now that they know the truth. Paige has no idea how lucky she is. She could've easily been dragged down, too. She hated Dane."

"She was never a suspect," Gary said.

"Why not? You never told me that."

"Think about it. Both victims were strangled. Do you know how hard it is to strangle someone? It's nothing like the movies. It takes forever. Paige is tough, but she's not that strong, even with a rope. And Otto had a blow to the head. I think that was just for show. James wanted to make it look messier than it was, more violent. More like a crime of passion by Dane McKenny. Supposedly."

Maggie pulled up a chair and sat down. "And another thing. Agnes Krueger gave you Paige Colpot's name and info. She sent you chasing a red herring. Isn't that interfering with an investigation? Shouldn't she be in trouble for that? Instead, she's hogging all the credit like you didn't do anything and the Fair Haven PD is useless."

"Does the article say the Fair Haven PD is useless?"

"No. But that's what she's implying."

"That's how *you're* interpreting it. I'm not. I'm just glad Thomas James is off the street. And that Serafina Lawson is safe. She almost gave him a ride to Virginia. He would've gotten away. Who knows what might've happened to her. She seems like a really nice woman."

"She is. I wish I was more like her."

"How do you mean?"

"My gosh, Gary. You'd have to be blind not to notice. She's at least two decades older than me, but she wears those amazing outfits, writes saucy stories, and has men following her around like puppies. You should have seen poor Trent when she told him he couldn't travel with her."

"I interviewed him at the hotel. You can't actually feel sorry for that guy," Gary said.

"He was smitten. To use Fifi's word."

"He was a gold-digger." Gary smirked.

Maggie looked at Gary, mouth hanging open. "Was he really?"

"Yes. Fifi knew. She kept him around to scare off the other gold-diggers."

"How do you know all this?"

"She told me when I interviewed her at the hotel. Remember when she and Trent disappeared upstairs? Supposedly to grab you a copy of her book? I had to know what was going on. She said it was all for show. She let him come along to look the part, but she hadn't even kissed him, except maybe on the cheek."

Maggie stared at Gary. "You're not lying to me? Not making fun of my naivety?"

"No, of course not. Besides, I like your naivety. And not picking up on something weird doesn't make you naive. People are weird," Gary said, yawning.

"Getting tired?" she asked.

"Yeah. They keep giving me stuff to make me sleepy when all I want is to stay awake and get out of here. Hospitals are the worst place to recuperate."

"Go ahead and close your eyes. I'll keep first watch," Maggie joked.

"You know you don't have to stay. Go home, sleep in your own bed. No one's going to mess with me here. The uniformed cops stop by every couple of hours to check in and make me laugh because they know it hurts." He rubbed his side with a smile.

"I know I don't have to stay. But you'd stay if it were me," she said, taking his hand.

"No, I wouldn't. I'd be at the nurse's station flirting and strutting around in my uniform. You know how girls love a man in uniform. And now I've got scars, too. Chicks dig scars." he grinned, nodding as he yawned again.

"Yeah, a scarred man in uniform who falls asleep by eight. That's what really gets them," Maggie chuckled.

Gary laughed—then winced. "I told you to quit being funny."

"I'll quit being funny when you quit being funny-looking."

"That's stupid," he said, laughing as his eyelids drooped.

"Then why are you laughing?"

Gary gave one last snort before sleep overtook him. Maggie kept holding his hand, resting her head on her arm. She only meant to rest her eyes, but she slipped into a deep sleep. She'd barely left Gary's side since he was admitted, only going home to shower and change. If she'd been gone more than ninety minutes in total, it was a lot. All the rushing had caught up to her.

That's why she never saw or heard Joshua when he quietly slipped in.

Had she been awake, she would've seen the

bouquet of flowers he brought for Gary and the get-well card. She would've seen the single rose meant for her.

When Maggie finally opened her eyes, holding Gary's hand, she noticed the flowers and the card. As she stretched, Gary woke up too.

"Yikes. You're still here?" he grumbled.

"That's exactly what I was thinking," she shot back. "Oh, how nice. You got a card and flowers from Joshua. I wonder when he showed up."

"You know," Gary said, "if I were picking a guy for you, aside from someone as awesome as myself, good luck finding that, I'd say Joshua's a good one."

Maggie's heart leapt, but she only rubbed her face and tried to shake off sleep.

"Hmm... I never thought of that," she lied but smiled.

About the Author

Harper Lin is a 3x *USA TODAY* bestselling cozy mystery author. When she's not reading or writing mysteries, she loves going to yoga classes, hiking, and baking with her family and friends.

For a complete list of her books by series, visit her website.

www.HarperLin.com

www.ingramcontent.com/pod-product-compliance
Lightning Source LLC
Chambersburg PA
CBHW022108240626
47153CB00007B/2283